"You May Stay, Phoebe."

Cain's deep baritone voice riddled Phoebe with sudden sharp memories. She ignored them. "How magnanimous of you," she snapped, wanting him to face her. "But no thanks. It's obvious no one is welcome here. I'll make other arrangements."

It was humiliating that she needed a place to hide. It wasn't in her nature to back down, but she was desperate to keep her life from spiraling out of control…again.

"Phoebe." His sharp tone demanded her attention.

She went still, her heart in her throat. "What?"

"Forgive my reluctance," he said softly. "I'd be… delighted if you'd stay at Nine Oaks."

That sounded about as welcoming as a case of the plague, Phoebe thought. "How about you look at me and say that? Then I might believe you."

Cain stiffened then turned his head. His gaze slammed into hers. Nine years tumbled away, and they were again naked, skin to skin. Wanting the contact to be more intimate.

Phoebe tried to push those memories away. She didn't need sensual distraction. She needed peace and privacy. And Nine Oaks was the only place she'd find them.

Dear Reader,

Sit back, relax and indulge yourself with all the fabulous offerings from Silhouette Desire this October. Roxanne St. Claire is penning the latest DYNASTIES: THE ASHTONS with *The Highest Bidder.* Youngest Ashton sibling, Paige, finds herself participating in a bachelorette auction and being "won" by a sexy stranger. Strangers also make great protectors, as demonstrated by Annette Broadrick in *Danger Becomes You,* her most recent CRENSHAWS OF TEXAS title.

Speaking of protectors, Michelle Celmer's heroine in *Round-the-Clock Temptation* gets a bodyguard of her very own: a member of the TEXAS CATTLEMAN'S CLUB. Linda Conrad wraps up her miniseries THE GYPSY INHERITANCE with *A Scandalous Melody.* Will this mysterious music box bring together two lonely hearts? For something a little darker, why not try *Secret Nights at Nine Oaks* by Amy J. Fetzer? A handsome recluse, an antebellum mansion—two great reasons to stay indoors. And be sure to catch Heidi Betts's *When the Lights Go Down,* the story of a plain-Jane librarian out to make some serious changes in her humdrum love life.

As you can see, Silhouette Desire has lots of great stories for you to enjoy. So spend this first month of autumn cuddled up with a good book—and come back next month for even more fabulous reads.

Enjoy!

Melissa Jeglinski

Melissa Jeglinski
Senior Editor
Silhouette Desire

Please address questions and book requests to:
Silhouette Reader Service
U.S.: 3010 Walden Ave., P.O. Box 1325, Buffalo, NY 14269
Canadian: P.O. Box 609, Fort Erie, Ont. L2A 5X3

Secret Nights
at Nine Oaks
Amy J. Fetzer

Published by Silhouette Books

America's Publisher of Contemporary Romance

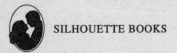 **SILHOUETTE BOOKS**

ISBN 0-373-76685-8

SECRET NIGHTS AT NINE OAKS

Copyright © 2005 by Amy J. Fetzer

This edition published by arrangement with Harlequin Books S.A.

Visit Silhouette Books at www.eHarlequin.com

Printed in U.S.A.

AMY J. FETZER

was born in New England and raised all over the world. She uses her own experiences in creating the characters and settings for her novels. Married more than twenty years to a United States Marine, and the mother of two sons, Amy covets the moments when she can curl up with a cup of cappuccino and a good book.

For the Henkels
Ryan, Mia and Miles

Family made us related
Life made us friends

Love you
Amy

One

Nine Oaks Plantation, SC

Cain Blackmon coveted his home and his privacy. So much so that he paid a fortune to keep people away from his estate. *People* should have included his younger sister, Suzannah.

The woman could drive a saint to violence.

She'd asked a favor; for the impossible. Not for him to leave Nine Oaks, that he wouldn't do, even for her, but to invite someone inside. To live. For *weeks*.

And that someone was Phoebe DeLongpree.

She might as well have dared him to name his most erotic fantasy and lay it out for the world to see.

"No." From a seat at his desk, Cain picked up a file. "There are plenty of hotels and spas in the area."

Suzannah blinked. "Well, that's just plain rude."

Cain didn't have any compunction about turning her down. He did not want that particular woman here.

Suzannah stepped nearer, her hands on her trim hips as she gave him a glare he remembered from their childhood. It signaled she was about to clamp down on a bone and refuse to let go. "This is my house, too, you know."

"Fine. When shall I expect your share of the restoration mortgage?"

"You're avoiding the issue."

"And you are refusing to accept the inevitable. I made myself very clear, Suzannah. I don't want a houseguest." Glancing at the closed door, he could almost scent Phoebe on the other side.

"You don't want *anyone* here, and for no good reason." He shot her a hard look and his sister wilted a little. "Fine—for reasons you won't discuss with *me*."

Her wounded tone gave Cain no more than a pinprick of regret, yet he looked to the painted ceiling with its intricately layered molding and prayed for patience. "All right, Suzannah. Tell me why I should invite a stranger—"

"She's not a stranger."

No, he thought, she was Phoebe. Shapely, sexy-without-trying Phoebe. A man's erotic vision in a five-foot-two package of sensuality and combustible energy. He knew her from firsthand experience when she'd rocketed through his life and this house once before, briefly, but long enough to stir his desire to dangerous heights. Enough that he'd caught her under the servants' staircase and kissed her.

It had been one of the most electric, sensual moments of his life. And a mistake. She'd been liquid fire in his arms, dragging him into her unstoppable passion. And scaring him with it. Yes, Cain admitted with a bit of youthful recollection. Scaring him. Because one touch told him he'd delved into something that would consume him whole.

The memory of it tightened his groin, and he shoved out of the chair, turned to the window and brushed back the curtain. He stared at the landscape that hadn't changed in over two hundred years, his gaze flowing over the familiar live oaks draped in Spanish moss, the manicured gardens sloping toward the boats floating lazily down the river. The serenity of it didn't stop the memory of a single warm, wet kiss that left him raw and stripped.

Cain pinched the bridge of his nose, thinking that

Lily had never made him feel even a degree of what he'd shared with Phoebe in those few moments.

And he'd married Lily.

His expression darkened, the memory of his late wife compounding the guilt he stacked in a corner of his mind. He didn't want to share his isolation for the simple reason that Phoebe would end up hating him, and he didn't want that burden.

"I'm listening," he prompted, impatient to say no, again.

"She'd dated this guy three times, called it quits, but he wouldn't go away. Then he got mean."

Cain twisted a look back over his shoulder, frowning. "Go on."

"It was Randall Kreeg, the fifth."

Cain's brows shot up as the realization set in. Randall Kreeg, the son of the CEO of Kreeg Enterprises. A computer-generated imaging company all filmmakers used today. He'd seen a news report, yet hadn't paid it much attention, nor had he associated Phoebe with P.A. DeLong. Like most, he assumed this person was a man. "He's been arrested as I recall."

"Yes. She'll testify against him in a few weeks. But that wasn't the half of it." When he frowned, she asked, "Don't you read the papers?"

"Yes, several, daily."

"Phoebe is P.A. DeLong. The film writer?"

Good God, he thought. Sweet little Phoebe wrote those terrifying scripts?

"I see you understand. Add to that, the L.A. press twisted the whole mess, accusing her of staging it for publicity and ignoring the fact that Kreeg terrorized her."

Cain tried to imagine someone entering his life just to torment him. He almost laughed. What was Phoebe but a walking torture for him? "He's in jail, then she's safe."

"For how long? He can post any bail, and with his high-priced lawyers, who do you think they'll smear? She had to leave L.A., but the press has dogged her since she landed here. Though she covers it well, she's this far—" Suzannah pinched the air between her thumb and forefinger "—from collapsing from exhaustion."

Exhaustion? Phoebe? The woman had more energy than ten people, which made him doubt his sister's viewpoint on the matter. He faced the window again, unwilling to concede to her demands. Then he heard the door open.

"Enough, 'Zannah! Stop!"

Cain recognized Phoebe's voice instantly.

"I won't have you begging him for this, for pity sake."

"You heard?" Suzannah said, clearly mortified.

"I didn't press my ear to the door since my mama taught me better, but his answer was *quite* clear."

Good, it saved him from repeating himself, Cain thought, his gaze on the view, hands clasped behind his back. He didn't turn to look at Phoebe. He didn't have to. The energy level in the room went up a couple notches the instant she stepped inside. To look at her now, well, that was like anticipating a mortal blow. He knew it was coming, and there was no doubt it would have more impact than he expected.

Yet Cain knew when he was licked. Suzannah would never forgive him if he denied her request. He had so few people in his life, and he adored his baby sister. He didn't want to lose her, too. So, he said the words that would leave him in complete agony for the next few weeks.

"You may stay, Phoebe."

His deep baritone voice riddled Phoebe with sudden sharp memories. She ignored them. "How magnanimous of you, my lord," she snapped. "But no thanks. It's obvious no one is welcome here. I'll make other arrangements." Though she didn't know where. The press had a sixth sense, and had already forced her across the country and out of Suzannah's place.

It was humiliating enough that she needed a place to hide. It wasn't in her nature to back down, but she was desperate to keep her life from spiraling out of control again. Cutting herself off from the world that had been very unfriendly to her lately was the only way. She'd lost so much and needed it back or she wouldn't be able to recognize herself in the mirror.

She was ready to leave, wanting to pinch Suzannah when she kept appealing to him.

"Phoebe." His sharp tone demanded her attention.

She went still, her heart in her throat. "What?"

"Forgive my reluctance," he said a little more softly. "I'd be…delighted if you'd stay at Nine Oaks."

That sounded about as welcoming as a case of the plague, Phoebe thought, moving a step closer. "How about you look at me and say that? Then I might believe you."

Cain stiffened, then turned his head. His gaze slammed into hers. Nine years tumbled away. They were trapped under the staircases, pawing at each other like teenagers, wanting contact to be tighter, more intimate. Naked, skin to skin. When she moved closer and met his gaze, he felt ashamed that he'd hurt her that next morning. But where Phoebe was concerned, going cold turkey was the only way to deal with something that powerful.

It was the hardest thing he'd ever done. Because he'd wanted her like breath itself.

Green eyes pleaded with him for understanding. The same way she'd looked at him that morning, yet never asked for an explanation. Her look drove into him like a punch. My God, she was beautiful. Nine years had aged her from a girl to a breathtaking woman. Dark red hair framed her face in uncontrolled layers, much like her personality. The wild cut suited her, framed her elfin face, her big innocent eyes. His gaze lowered unconsciously to her mouth, to the lushest lips he'd ever had the pleasure to kiss and for a second he remembered the exotic taste of her. His gaze drifted lower, over her body wrapped in a frilly rust-colored top and matching leather skirt that was short enough to be illegal. Sexy without trying, he thought, catching a hint of something lacy under the sheer blouse. Right now he wanted nothing more than to be consumed by his own desire for her again. See if it had been a fabrication of his youth or still as real as his memories. He shoved the thought down. He couldn't afford to think or feel any of that. Not ever. Not for her.

"If it's refuge you seek, then Nine Oaks is at your disposal."

Phoebe wasn't listening. She was staring. He was bigger than she remembered, taller, broader in the shoulders. The pale sunlight shimmering through the windows silhouetted him against the sheer curtains, making his rich brown hair shine, the angled cut of his jaw stand out against his pristine white dress shirt. He gave off an aura of isolation, yet when he faced her fully, Phoebe couldn't breathe as his dark eyes clashed with hers.

Intense, assessing, edged with anger.

His mysterious hooded look was nothing like the man of her past, and the way he scrutinized her from head to toe made her feel peeled open and vulnerable. She smoothed her leather skirt and didn't like that he made her nervous.

But then, she was getting an opportunity that hundreds of people would kill for. A look at the South's most infamous recluse. He didn't look it, though. She wasn't expecting long hair and pale skin or anything like that, yet he looked…well, as heart-stoppingly handsome as he had nine years ago, but now, there was a dark gloom surrounding him. While it was sexy and mystifying, it made her want to pull apart the reasons he hid from the world. Even hid from his sister.

"*Is* that what you want?" he said, startling her.

Phoebe tried gathering her thoughts when she could taste the strain in the air. She knew the truth. He *really* didn't want her staying here. Normally, she'd have taken the hint and split. She wasn't dense, but she *was* desperate. Her life was in shambles and there was no sign that the press would leave her alone until the trial weeks away. She needed peace and privacy. To feel safe again.

"Yes," she said. "Just for a little while." She needed time to get a handle on her insomnia and, hopefully, regain her creativity.

"Do you have your things with you now?" he asked.

"No. To be honest, I didn't anticipate a yes."

Cain's brows knitted. His gaze moved to his sister standing behind Phoebe, her arms folded, a warning in her eyes. *Don't hurt her,* Suzannah was saying. *You've done that already.* He must be reading that wrong, Cain thought. Surely Suzannah didn't know about that kiss. But then, Phoebe and her sister had been friends for over a dozen years. They probably told each other everything. All the more reason to keep away from Phoebe while she was here.

Then Suzannah said, "Since I'm leaving for England," on business for him, Cain knew, "she'll be here this afternoon."

"Would you like me to send a limousine for you?" Cain offered, reaching for the phone.

Phoebe blinked. "Good grief, no. I wouldn't know how to behave in one."

"Not alone, at least," Suzannah muttered, a secret smile passing between the women. Phoebe's cheeks pinkened delicately, and Cain was instantly jealous of the man who'd had the pleasure of misbehaving with Phoebe inside a dark luxurious car.

Oblivious to the images rushing through his brain, Phoebe pushed Suzannah out the door ahead of her, then paused to look back around the edge. She met his gaze across the large room. "I appreciate this, Cain. I'll see you this afternoon."

No, you won't, he thought, yet nodded just the same.

The electronic sensors on the front gates sounded softly from Cain's computers, the relay reminding him of his promise to his sister. He'd thought of little else since this morning. His offer to Phoebe was gallant, but a mistake.

Cain pinched the bridge of his nose, then looked at the screen. Video cameras were positioned around the property, each one representing a separate block on the monitor. In the upper left square, Phoebe sat behind the wheel of a topless yellow Jeep, waving frantically at the camera, then looking behind herself. Her panic was full-blown, and the sudden urge to protect her shot through him.

Quickly hitting another key, he opened the gates

and she shot through with little room to spare. The gates closed behind her and he aimed the camera down the street to show a TV news van skidding to a halt. Photographers leaped out, snapping pictures. His irritation made him hit the speaker. "You are on private property. Please leave."

The man and woman looked startled. "It's a public road, pal."

"I *own* the road. The gates are now armed."

To bring the matter home, the Dobermans raced to the gate, their fangs and bark sending the couple into the van.

Unaffected, Cain turned from the console. Suzannah hadn't given him details of what Kreeg had done to Phoebe, and he suspected his sister was protecting her friend any way she could. Even from him. After Phoebe and Suzannah had left, Cain had done a search for any information. As much as the press was hounding her, it had more on Phoebe than on the police capture and Kreeg. The thought of her being hunted and tormented made Cain's anger rise.

Trying to distract himself from the woman racing up his driveway, Cain grabbed a sheaf of papers, and began making notes he really didn't comprehend. Temptation won and he glanced at the screen. She looked…well, comfortable in her own skin, he thought, dark red hair flying, her plush body in a tight tank top and jean skirt that hugged her delicious curves as she shot up the drive at full speed.

It didn't surprise him. She'd always been a bit untamed. That was the reason he hadn't pursued her after that kiss under the stairs. All that energy was dangerous. A strand of unwanted regret laced through him like a rope about to tighten, choking him. With more force than necessary, Cain tapped the intercom console. "Benson?"

"I saw her, sir."

Benson was always one step ahead of everyone, including Cain. "See that Miss DeLongpree has everything she needs."

"Yes sir. Will you be meeting with her, sir?"

"No." She wouldn't be pleased about that, but subjecting Phoebe to his lifestyle was out of the question.

She'd asked for sanctuary.

Nine Oaks was a fortress, his private haven from the public eye. From anyone. For five years.

If Phoebe DeLongpree wanted solitude, then he'd give it to her. Only that. He'd already ruined one woman's life. He wouldn't take the chance of destroying another one.

Phoebe sped past two-hundred-year-old oak trees lining the nearly mile-long private lane to the house, their branches arching over the road like protective arms, welcoming her into seclusion. Into the ancestral home of Augustus Cain Blackmon the fourth. A bona fide recluse.

No one, including his sister, understood why he did the Howard Hughes thing, but there was a lot of speculation about why he hadn't shown himself in public or private since the death of his wife five years ago.

Though Cain never discussed his reasons with anyone, Suzannah believed it was because he loved his wife so much that he was still mourning her. But Phoebe, being a scriptwriter, came up with a dozen, slightly twisted scenarios, none of them as touching as a man who couldn't face the world without his bride. A real waste of a good-looking man, in her opinion.

In nine years, Cain Blackmon had aged to perfection, yet looks aside, why he cut himself off from the world nudged at her curiosity. Why lock himself up when he didn't have to? She'd have gone nuts being so confined. Besides, the newspapers had stopped asking why a couple years ago. At the thought of the press, she glanced in the rearview mirror as the news van pulled away. She understood Cain's need for privacy.

Sometimes, being alone was a good thing.

She wasn't used to publicity, either. Using the pseudonym of P.A. DeLong and being anonymous had suited her just fine.

Randall Kreeg had changed all that.

Needles of fear pricked her spine and she glanced in the rearview mirror again, half expecting to see him sitting behind her, looking smug and arrogant. Then she realized that no one stepped on this property without Cain's permission. *He can't touch me here,* she reminded herself and gripping the steering wheel, she worked her shoulders, refusing to allow her fear to ruin this opportunity to retrieve her creativity.

Yes, being alone was a good thing for her now.

Just not five years of it. Granted, Cain's seclusion was overkill in her opinion, but then she wasn't Cain. She'd never loved anyone that much. And she didn't have Nine Oaks to escape to. Till now.

As the house came into view, she felt as if she were in a time warp. Rolling to a stop in front of the antebellum mansion, she locked the brake and stood on the seat of her Jeep, then braced her arms on the top of the windshield. She just stared.

It hadn't changed in about two hundred years, if she had to hazard a guess. Suzannah told her that Cain had had the entire plantation restored to its former glory, even the stables. Porches wrapped the upper and lower levels of the mansion, a widow's walk was on the third floor. Painted white and trimmed with Charleston green shutters so dark they looked black, the house rambled, its stone verandas leading to a dock, the river and a pool. From the river, acres of land spread out in three directions opening on to fruit orchards, rice, sugar, peanuts, cotton and timber. While pictures of Nine Oaks graced local shops, hotels and restaurants, nothing compared to seeing it up close again.

She loved this house. Its serene elegance drew her. Suzannah had always brushed off Phoebe's awe and envy over Nine Oaks, but then she'd grown up here with Cain. For a second, she wondered where he was. The library again, she decided, her gaze skimming the house.

The front doors opened, and while she didn't expect Cain, she was a little disappointed when a young man dressed in a white shirt and dark slacks trotted down the steps. Another man, older and wearing a suit, walked sedately behind the first.

The young man smiled brightly. "I'm Willis, Miss DeLongpree. I'll take your bags up for you and park your car."

She thanked him, smiling as she pitched him the keys, cautioning him the second gear stuck a little. Silver haired and slender, the older man waited on the wide Federal staircase and Phoebe recognized him as she mounted the first few steps.

"Hello, Benson," she said. "How's it going?".

Not a fraction of Benson's distinguished expression changed as he nodded and said, "Miss DeLongpree. Welcome back to Nine Oaks."

"Thanks." Just because she knew it would fluster him, she popped up and kissed his cheek. "You're looking mighty good there, darlin'."

He blinked and cleared his throat, his ears glowing pink. "And you, miss."

"You still riding roughshod over the gang here?"

His eyes twinkled. "I will die doing just that, ma'am."

Phoebe had the urge to tickle him just to see if he knew how to smile. She liked him. Once, Suzannah had snitched liquor from her daddy's private stock and together they'd indulged too much. Benson had found them, drunk and silly, and managed to get them both to Suzannah's room before anyone discovered their crime. Then he went beyond the call, soothing their hangovers with some old-fashioned remedy, and never telling a soul. *You had to love a man who knew how to be discreet.*

Following him, she stepped into the coolness of the house, looking around at the familiar decor. Heart-pine floors stretched for yards in three directions, complementing the pale yellow walls and the carved pecan wood moldings and doors. But the real eye catcher was the twin sweeping wood staircases that led to the second and third floors of the east and west wings. *Eat your heart out, Scarlett.*

She looked at Benson. "So where's Cain?"

"Mr. Blackmon is very busy. Follow me, please." He headed for the stairs.

"Too busy to greet his guest?"

"He's aware you've arrived, Miss Phoebe."

Of that she didn't doubt, yet Phoebe stopped where she was and Benson paused on the stairs, looking down at her, then arching a brow. "Not even a hello?"

Sympathy clouded his dark eyes. "Mr. Blackmon doesn't receive visitors."

"He really is the ogre locked in his castle, isn't he?" Somehow, she'd hoped his extremeness was mostly rumor.

Benson's gaze narrowed, and in a heartbeat he went from majordomo to watchdog. "He does as he pleases, miss."

"Yes, well, so do I."

Phoebe turned to her left and walked toward the library, suspecting he was in there. Cain didn't owe her a thing—if he was going to ignore her, fine, he could. It was his house. But nine years ago, the man had kissed her into a bone-melting puddle, and now they were connected.

He owed her at least a "Hello, how's your mama?"

"Miss DeLongpree. I wouldn't advise opening that door."

Lord, he sounded afraid for her. "Duly noted, Benson. I take full responsibility."

She pushed it open and stepped into the grand library. She hadn't really taken notice of it this morning, yet her gaze landed first on the back walls lined with dark wood shelves and stuffed tight with leather-bound books. Her mouth practically watered. There were groupings of chairs, and antiques dotted the room. Rich heart-pine floors were covered with vivid carpets in a mix of burgundy, blue and gold. Masculine, opulent, the room spoke of aged brandy and Cuban cigars, soft conversations about finance and world affairs. It said *Cain,* she thought, quiet, reserved. For a second, she absorbed the history lingering like smoke inside the walls before looking around the room again.

He wasn't there.

The chair was turned away from the desk, and a bank of computer screens filled one side of a large U-shaped work center. On the bottom of one of the computer screens, the stock market updates ticked by. Yet aside from the usual desk paraphernalia, lamp, phones, blotter, there was a china cup and saucer.

And whatever was in it, was still steaming.

He'd heard her coming and left somehow.

Phoebe felt a hard punch somewhere near her heart.

She didn't bother looking further. Quietly, she backed out and closed the door. Benson didn't say a word, didn't show any emotion, but Phoebe suddenly felt like the morning after Cain had kissed her so thoroughly, then later behaved as if it had never happened.

She felt ignored. Unworthy. Used.

Disappointed, she followed Benson upstairs.

Two

A half hour later, Benson slipped into the library, posting himself at the edge of Cain's desk.

"Is she settled?" Cain asked, writing.

"As well as Miss DeLongpree can settle, sir."

Cain looked up, amused. "Still a little hyper?"

"Yes, sir. She's in the east wing, the yellow suite," Benson said. He added, "She was very determined to see you."

Cain said nothing, closing a folder. He'd heard her coming and slipped out through a secret passageway his ancestors had built into this house over a century ago to escape from the Union Army. It was devious and a bit cowardly, but Cain told himself he was sparing Phoebe. He wasn't the man she knew before, and she'd be expecting that.

"Where is she now?"

Benson gestured to the security screen, to the center block, and Cain watched as Phoebe, in a bikini, hopped on the diving board.

"Oh good God." His muscles locked, heat skimming his bloodstream. Cain swallowed. There wasn't enough bikini to cover that body, he thought, and watched her bounce on the board, then jackknife and plunge head first into the twenty-foot-deep water. She barely made a splash.

"Impressive," Benson said, and Cain spared him a glance. If he didn't know better, he'd swear the man was smiling.

Seconds later, she popped to the surface in a smooth arch, then started swimming laps, looking like a slim, hot pink torpedo shooting through the water. Cain watched her for a second, then tapped the keys and viewed another section of the property. He wasn't a voyeur, but the image of her round plump breasts spilling out of her top left an imprint in his mind.

And in his blood.

It confirmed what he knew—getting anywhere near Phoebe was dangerous.

"She won't give up easily, sir."

Cain rubbed his temple. "She doesn't have a choice."

"Sir…if you would simply—"

"Spare me the sermon, Benson. Please."

Once in a while, Benson made a plea for him to leave Nine Oaks. Since Benson had practically raised him, he wasn't offended. Yet Benson had been here the day his wife had died. He'd heard the horrible argument they'd had, had warned him when Lily had taken a boat out onto the river.

Cain didn't choose to be alone because he was grieving, as most people assumed.

He was alone, because he was paying for his crime.

Lily wasn't skilled enough to sail alone.

And that night, he knew it.

There was a fine art to being lazy.

Phoebe hadn't a clue how to begin. As a kid, her mom had instilled in her that "a flagrant misuse of time" was nothing short of criminal. Once Phoebe was on her own, she'd gotten over that. Well, mostly.

She'd always been a little hyperactive, which translated into her mouth running faster than her brain and getting her and Suzannah into major trouble when they were in college. But she'd needed to do something, even if it was wrong. Right now, she wished for anything so she could sleep tonight. After weeks without a good night's rest, the reflection in the mirror was looking pretty sad. She dreaded bedtime.

Although she could have done another twenty laps, she was waterlogged already. Maybe later, she thought, trying to clear her ears as she stepped inside the house. Maybe after one of Jean Claude's famous meals.

Entering the house from the south side, she wrapped the flowered sarong more securely around her hips and headed toward the foyer. Her heeled sandals clicked on the pinewood floors, almost echoing in the big house. The sound made her feel as if she were in a museum, that any extra noise was going to earn a reprimand from the guard.

That would be Benson, she thought, smiling. She passed several unused rooms, and knew she and Cain were the only people here who didn't work for the estate. It was sad to have so much room and not use it. The house screamed for a big summer party.

Suddenly she found herself staring at the library door. She hadn't meant to come this way, especially not dressed as she was. But Cain was in there. She could hear the low murmur of his voice. She thought about how he'd slipped out of the room when he knew she was coming in, and the sting of it skipped through her again. This need to see him irritated her. She didn't really want to speak to someone who went out of his way not to be near her, but just the same, the need was there. Being so casually dismissed pushed her to reach for the door latch. Her hand stopped midway. Whoever Cain was talking with, he didn't sound pleased.

When it grew quiet again, she rapped on the door. She heard his unintelligible response and pushed it open, her gaze sliding around the room, then focusing on the desk. He stood behind it, his hands clasped behind his back as he looked out the window. He stared at the water a lot, she realized.

"Yes, Benson?"

"It's me, Cain."

He stiffened, yet kept his back to her.

"What is it that you want?" Cain said more tersely than he intended.

She considered the wisdom of confronting him when clearly he didn't want her near. "Am I truly welcome here?"

Her voice sounded fragile, and Cain sighed softly and faced her. His gaze latched onto her face, to her pretty green eyes that looked so hollow right now. Then his attention slipped lower. Good God, he thought and swallowed, his pulse skipping a couple of beats. The skimpy bikini barely covered her smooth tanned skin while the sarong was tied low on her hips and showed the enticing dip of her navel. He'd never seen anything so exotic.

"Am I, Cain?"

He dragged his gaze to her face. "Of course you are."

She sagged a little. He didn't want to make her feel uninvited. He just didn't want her within touching distance. His moods had a tendency to rub off on people, and knowing she was here, simply reminded him that he'd made a terrible mistake before and would never risk it again. But the temptation just to look at her won out over his better judgment and Cain moved from behind the desk.

Phoebe watched his approach as if she were looking down a long thin tunnel. Her world narrowed. Cain. The man who'd made her world tilt years ago and never tip right since then. Her knees softened a little. Her tastes in men didn't normally lean to the suit-and-tie type, but lordy-my, a girl could change her taste, couldn't she? His white dress shirt pulled at his broad shoulders, his hair a dark, chocolate-brown that shone so much she wanted to run her fingers through it.

He stopped, and she looked up at him. "Thank you, Cain."

He only nodded. Silence stretched between them

and for a woman who normally didn't know how to shut up, she was at a loss for words. She tried for the ordinary.

"So are you going to have dinner with me or anything, or just keep this distance you're so fond of lately?"

"Perhaps."

That wasn't an answer. "Well, just so you know, I'm available for cocktails at five."

A smile barely curved his mouth. "I'll remember that."

Her gaze traveled over his face. "You're just so snappy with the pleasant conversation, aren't you?" Now that she was near him, her nervousness fled. Amazing, she thought. It was like staring into the face of someone she'd known for…centuries.

When he didn't say anything, kept staring, she said, "Out of practice?"

"Hardly."

"We can start at the beginning." She held out her hand. "Hi, I'm Phoebe DeLongpree, your sister's best friend."

He looked down at her hand. He knew what would happen if he touched her, felt her warm skin against his in something as mundane as a handshake. He'd want more, and that he couldn't have. Ever.

"Very funny."

Phoebe frowned, lowering her hand. "More than a physical recluse, I see." Miffed, she moved to the door.

"Phoebe."

"Yes?"

"This is a male household. I suggest you cover yourself a bit more."

Phoebe didn't bother looking down at herself. She knew what she looked like. She'd run nearly a hundred miles in the last couple weeks, worked out till she was sore and tired, doing anything to fall into a peaceful sleep. She faced him. He was behind his desk again, shuffling files.

"It's a bikini, Cain."

"Is that what you call that?" There was more cloth in a handkerchief than in that top, for heaven's sake. And unfortunately, Cain's imagination was easily filling in what lay beneath every sparse inch of fabric.

"Yes, I do. And I look good in it or I wouldn't be wearing it. And anyone on your staff could have walked outside and seen me, so I think the problem lies with *you*."

He snapped a look at her. She unwrapped the sarong, slinging it over her shoulder, and on heeled sandals the same shade as her bikini, she turned and walked to the door.

His gaze lowered and Cain groaned, feeling mortally wounded. The damn thing was a thong, and her slim hips and tight, round behind rocked in sexy motion as she left his office. He closed his eyes, the image replaying in his mind enough to make his ears ring and every muscle in his body lock up. His groin was so tight he thought he'd snap in two if he tried to sit.

Cain let out a long-suffering breath, rubbing his face, then scraping his hands back over his skull.

As much as he wanted her gone, he wouldn't go back on his promise. When he lowered gingerly into the chair, he resigned himself to the sexiest creature on the planet torturing him with temptation.

It was going to be weeks of pure hell.

Standing at the top of the staircase, Phoebe eyed the long curving banister, imagining descending the steps in a gown to a handsome escort waiting at the bottom. Chewing her lip, she leaned out, looking down the halls to see if she was alone, then hitched her rear onto the polished banister and slid her way down. She hopped to the floor, her sneakers squeaking, and she did a little wiggle before turning toward the hall.

Someone cleared his throat.

She flinched, spinning around. Willis stood nearby, grinning, and holding a tray. Phoebe flushed a little, put her finger to her lips, then moved closer.

"This is for Cain, right?" she said, scoping out the coffee service.

"Yes, ma'am."

She snatched the pad and pencil from the breast pocket of his jacket, and scribbled a note, then stuffed it under the saucer. Willis, blond and young, gave the plate a skeptical look.

If that won't get a rise out of Cain, nothing will, she thought, then winked at Willis before heading toward the heavenly scent of freshly baked bread.

Benson appeared out of nowhere. "Miss Phoebe, dinner is served." He gestured toward the formal dining room.

"Oh, great." She was looking forward to tasting one of Jean Claude's creations. She followed Benson into the dining room, its vivid red walls and white trim giving a casual feel to the austere surroundings. The older man pulled out her chair and when she sat, he lifted silver domes off the plates. Her mouth watered as the glorious scents of lemon, chicken and delicate vegetables wafted up to greet her.

She tipped in her chair, looking around. "Cain isn't joining me?"

"No, miss."

"Well, that stinks," she muttered under her breath.

Benson poured her some wine and offered her napkin, then said, "Enjoy," before he left her alone.

Phoebe stared at the wide empty room. "Hello, hello, hello," she said like an echo. She hated eating alone. It was boring and she always ate too fast. She felt a bit insulted that Cain couldn't be bothered to join her. She'd practically invited him to, in his own house no less.

Gathering her plate and utensils in the napkin, she walked to the kitchen, stopping in the doorway, and taking in the small bit of chaos. The Nine Oaks' kitchen had been modernized and she didn't know what half the appliances were used for, but then, a microwave was her best friend lately.

Around the edge of the granite counter, a few of the staff sat, eating dinner and watching the TV. She recognized Jean Claude, Willis and Mr. Dobbs, who handled the dogs and cared for the stables. The two others she hadn't met yet, but from the looks of their clothing, they worked on the grounds.

"Oh, I could just live at your feet, Jean Claude," she said, inhaling deeply. "You could just throw me some scraps and I'd be grateful."

Jean Claude glanced her way as he pulled a flat wooden paddle filled with steaming loaves of bread out of the stone oven. "Well, where y'at, Miss Phoebe?" His smile was big and bright.

"I'm just fine, Jean Claude. Do y'all mind if I join

you?" She nodded toward the counter. "It's dull eating with a flower arrangement for company."

"Yes, of course," the group said, and Willis hopped up to get her plate and make a spot for her.

She slid onto a stool at the granite counter.

"I was glad to hear you were coming for a visit, Miss Phoebe," Jean Claude said.

"Shocked you, I'll bet," she said, cutting her chicken. It was stuffed with crabmeat and shrimp and she was practically drooling over it before the first bite made it to her mouth.

His lips curved. "Yes'm, it did."

Jean Claude was raised in New Orleans, Cajun to the bone, tall, slim and handsome at nearly sixty. There was something terribly sexy about a man who could cook, and Jean Claude was the best chef in five counties.

"Suzannah invited me. I think she blackmailed Cain, though."

"Miss 'Zannah is a strong woman, that I'll say."

"I'd say pushy."

"More than you?"

She smiled. "She runs a close second." She gave him her best begging-to-try-it look. "You going to share some of that?" She eyed the fresh bread.

"What? You don't like my dinner?" He nodded toward the plate.

"It's great, but your bread, well…it's a spiritual thing."

Grinning, Jean Claude cut her a slice, slathering it with butter.

"Bless you, I was *so* prepared to grovel," she said, then sank her teeth into the warm bread and swore she'd just tripped into food heaven. The flavors of herbs and butter exploded in her mouth. "Divine, Jean Claude."

He flashed her a smooth smile, slicing and packaging up the remaining loaves as he introduced her to the others having dinner. The TV droned softly.

After a few minutes, the conversation grew lively as Jean Claude told stories of some of Phoebe and Suzannah's college antics. "I come down here, and they had the freezer wide open, and the two of them were sitting on the floor, eating ice cream. Just a spoonful here and there, mind you, but from every bucket I had." Jean Claude tsked and winked at her.

"We were bonding over both getting Ds on history term papers. But I paid for that ice cream with a stomachache for two days. But poor 'Zannah, she felt the need to go jogging." The group groaned, imagining the damage. "It wasn't pretty," Phoebe said.

"You would have been better served to study harder," Jean Claude said.

"Oh yeah, sure, but then, that would have been sensible."

"Did you pass the course?" a voice said from the doorway, and they all looked up.

Cain was leaning against the door frame and the room grew noticeably quiet. When Willis made to leave, Phoebe subtly put her hand on his arm, keeping him still. How long had he been standing there?

She tipped her chin up. "Yes I did. I didn't have much else to do but study for the exam with a stomachache. Your sister, however, didn't make higher than a C on the final."

"Tattletale," Cain said, amused.

"What are friends for?" She grinned hugely, then said, "You going to stand there or come join us?"

Cain recognized the challenge in her eyes. Everyone stared and waited. Never taking his gaze off her, he pushed off the door frame and came into the kitchen. Her triumphant smile was damned annoying.

"Sir, would you like your dinner now?" Jean Claude said.

"Sure he would," Phoebe said, nudging out a stool, and Cain hesitated before he sat beside her.

Jean Claude looked at him, waiting, and Cain nodded, too interested in feeling the heat of Phoebe's body, in smelling her perfume. It was intoxicating.

She was intoxicating. Dressed in a short denim skirt and a red top that scooped low enough to show come great cleavage, she looked fresh and incredibly desirable. But then, all Phoebe had to do was walk into a room and he was pretty much sunk.

Her note under the coffee service tray hadn't pulled him from his office, though her scribbled words *"Come out and play with me"* were evocative enough to give him daydreams for the rest of his life.

But he'd been drawn by the noise, the laughter that echoed down the hall. It had been a very long time since he'd heard that. He'd stood at the door for a couple of minutes, watching as Phoebe pulled everyone into the conversation, turning the focus off her and onto the men. She talked easily, smiled often, and looked right at home. But then she was the highlight of the house. Aside from his sister, there hadn't been a woman at Nine Oaks in five years. Cain's thoughts shifted to Lily and he instantly derailed them, unwilling to ruin his dinner.

Jean Claude served up a plate of dinner and Cain ate, listening as Phoebe told a joke. Laughing with them, one of the men said goodbye, and left.

"I saw you diving, Miss Phoebe," Willis said and Cain shot Phoebe a covert look. "You're very good. That jackknife was something else."

"Thank you, Willis."

For one pointed moment, she looked directly at Cain as if to say, "see, I told you so." But all Cain had on his mind was the sexy image of her prancing out of his office with her bare behind jiggling. He'd tried all day to banish that picture and failed. He sure as hell didn't need another reminder. His body wanted this woman. It damn near screamed when he was near her. And sitting beside her, feeling her arm brush his, was enough to shoot another wave of heat through his bloodstream. He was glad there were people around; he couldn't trust himself alone with her.

"I was on a team in college," Phoebe said. "Heck, I was on three. Track, 500-meter relay swimming, diving." She looked at the young man. "I've always been wound a little too tight."

"Well, there's a news flash," Cain said dryly, eating.

"No. Really?" Jean Claude put in and she laughed. "I'm surprised that you can sit still long enough to write."

She looked up, chewed, then swallowed. "You know?"

"We read the papers, *bébé*," Jean Claude said.

Cain felt a surge go through her, saw her shoulders go taut. He'd never seen her tense up so fast. And though he didn't know the details of the incident with Randall Kreeg, he decided it was time he found out more.

Phoebe glanced around at the group, flushing with embarrassment. "Yes, well, I guess the cat's out of the bag about that."

The sudden silence was interrupted by the TV and a news flash. Cain heard her name and looked up.

The broadcast recapped the arrest and incarceration of Kreeg and mentioned speculation that Phoebe or the last producer who'd bought her script had staged the incident. He looked at Phoebe. She was frozen, her attention riveted to the TV. He called to her, but she didn't respond.

All Phoebe saw was Kreeg, looking rich, handsome and so damn supreme as the police escorted him into the station. A wave of memories hit her, blanketing her thoughts, bringing back the terror of realizing that Kreeg had touched her things, had been in her car. Then in her house.

Her breathing quickened.

Beside her, Cain frowned, noticing her hands shake.

"Phoebe?" Cain called again.

She lifted her gaze to his and the scared look in her eyes fractured his heart.

And made it bleed.

Three

Cain laid his hand on her arm and she flinched, trembling, her gaze shooting around the room, panicked as if searching for an escape.

His features tightened, then he leaned closer, sliding his hand farther up her arm and whispering, "It's okay, darlin', you're safe here. I swear it."

Phoebe blinked, then let out a long, shaky breath, and looked at him. Her eyes were owlish wide, as if replaying the last seconds in her mind, and she looked so frail and small that Cain fought the urge to take her in his arms. Then just as quickly as it came, her fear vanished and her shoulders relaxed.

"Well, don't I feel stupid," she muttered, her cheeks pinkening.

Cain rubbed her arm. "It's all right." For a second she gripped his hand, holding his gaze, then suddenly self-conscious of their nearness, she let go and looked at the others.

"I know he's in jail, but…"

Jean Claude's expression fell. "Forgive me, Miss Phoebe." He shut off the TV.

Her gaze jerked to the chef's. "Oh Jean Claude, it's not your fault. Not at all." She waved, all bright smiles. "It's just me being a little neurotic." She released an uneasy laugh, then picked up her fork, spearing a piece of chicken.

Cain frowned. He'd never seen anyone so upset one minute, then fine the next. Or was she just smothering her anxiety for their sake? And what the hell did that bastard do to her to make her so afraid still?

"He can't hurt you here," Cain assured. "No one will."

"It's why I'm here." Phoebe shifted her gaze to his, smiling.

But Cain could tell it was forced, could see the shadows in her eyes. And right now, he wanted only to take up arms and battle her demons for her. It startled him, reminded him that it was wiser to stay clear of her. Cain didn't deserve to be around a woman like her.

Yet he stayed where he was, unable to leave.

Jean Claude went to put the loaves of bread in the pantry, and the rest of the staff departed quickly.

She looked around. "Well, I sure know how to clear a room, huh?"

"Not really. They're unaccustomed to dining with me," he confessed. "*Are* you all right?"

"Yeah sure, just great," she said cheerily, and started clearing dishes, not wanting to answer the questions she could see in his eyes. She'd been there too many times, with friends, the police, her parents. In her dreams. The fact that Kreeg could post any bail that was set and walk free never left her thoughts.

"I wouldn't do that," Cain warned, nodding toward the dishes. "You tread on sacred ground by invading his kitchen." To prove him right, Jean Claude had a fit when he came back and in thickly accented Cajun, he shooed them both out.

Cain was already at the door. "See, told you."

She mimicked him, making a face, then thanked Jean Claude and left the kitchen.

Cain was several steps ahead of her, and at the foyer, she stopped, realizing he'd just dismissed her from his mind. He confirmed it when he entered the library and closed the door. The sound echoed up the hall, and Phoebe wondered when he'd grown so un-feeling, then rethought that, recalling his comforting touch in the kitchen. She could still feel the warmth of his hand on her skin. But it felt as if he were running from her now.

What was it about her that made him so standoff-ish and cold? Their one moment of past history? Or was it something else? And what really made him re-treat into Nine Oaks and never leave?

Back at his desk, Cain focused on work, making calls to his plant and crop operations managers and reading over a half-dozen status reports. Anything to keep his thoughts focused when they were eas-ily distracted. With Phoebe. Knowing she was somewhere near.

Roaming. Being Phoebe. Driving him nuts.

Leaving his chair, he moved to the shelves of books and selected a ledger from last year. His gaze caught on a drawer he knew housed racks of DVDs and he opened it, scanning them for one film he knew P.A. DeLong had written. He popped it into the player, saw her pen name on the credits and kept watching.

A half hour later, he was in a chair, involved in the paranormal plot so twisted and tense, he gripped the armrests. He glanced at the clock, then shut it off, yet stared at the blank screen for a moment, thinking that maybe someone in Hollywood had put the word out that her assault was staged. Just the rumor would have been publicity enough. Or had Kreeg's lawyers done that? Phoebe's pseudonym suggested she didn't want to be known for her controversial work. She liked hiding behind it. The thought brought a smile as he returned to his desk.

But concentration eluded him. Was this to be the pattern of the next couple of weeks? He'd be bankrupt if he wasn't careful, he thought, shaking his head and plowing into work.

Sometime later, the intercom buzzed. "Sir?" Benson said. "Miss DeLongpree is outside."

Benson sounded a little tense, and Cain frowned, tapping the button. "She has free rein of the place, Benson."

"But it's dusk, sir. The dogs are out."

Cain cursed, leaving his chair, then flung open the French doors to the library and raced out onto the stone veranda. His gaze shot around the landscape.

The Dobermans were running across the side lawn at top speed with teeth bared. His attention shifted to the figure a good distance away and to his left.

He called her name, and Phoebe turned, waving. Cain ran, pushing himself faster, knowing if he didn't outdistance the dogs, the animals bred for defense would tear her to shreds.

"Phoebe, the dogs!"

She looked at the dogs running toward her and froze. Horror rocketed through him as the Dobermans leaped at her. They knocked her to the ground, pinning her.

Cain commanded the animals, but they merely hesitated, and sliding to his knees, he yanked at the dog's collars.

Then he heard Phoebe laugh and focused.

The dogs weren't attacking. They were licking her face.

She giggled. "All right, guys, you weigh a ton, back off." Still the dogs nuzzled her, tails wagging like whips in the air.

This time, Cain shouted a command at the dogs, and the pair of black Dobermans jumped back and sat still.

Instantly, he ran his hands over her damp face, shoulders, her bare legs.

"You're trying to use this as an excuse to feel me up, right?"

Braced over her, he ignored her teasing, then demanded, "They didn't bite you?"

"No. They were greeting me."

"Greeting!" he roared.

"Yeah. That and they wanted these." She held up her hand, filled with half-crushed dog biscuits. "Scooby snacks," she said, grinning.

Cain fell back on his haunches and scraped a hand through his hair. The second he caught his breath, he tore into her. "How could you be so damn stupid!"

She hitched up on her elbows. "I beg your pardon?"

"They could have torn you to pieces! They could have killed you!"

"If I ran, sure, which is why I didn't." She frowned at him. He was breathing hard and looking as if *he'd* like to chew her to shreds. "You forgot that Suzannah and I slept with these dogs when they were puppies. They remembered me."

"It's been a very long time, Phoebe," he said, pulling her off the ground as he stood. He grasped her shoulders and for a moment he simply stared down at her. *She could have been mauled,* echoed through his mind and somewhere in his chest, muscles clenched. He'd rather die than see her hurt, and without his will, his gaze lowered to her mouth. Ripe and painted rose-pink.

Tempting him.

She met his gaze and his pulse pounded. The woman had too much control over him. She made him feel like a feral animal too long in the wild and a deep, troubling hunger lanced through him, the pressure of it settling hotly in his groin. It clamored for satisfaction, for release. For her. Yet he knew without being inside her, without having tasted more than her mouth, that it wouldn't be enough. He'd never wanted a woman more.

He knew that nine years ago, *and* the instant she stepped into his domain again. Then she tipped her head back, her gaze locking with his and Cain felt himself sinking. He bent, his mouth nearing hers. They were a breath away when the impact of what he was doing hit him.

Cain let her go and stepped back. "You took a big chance that they'd remember you."

Phoebe frowned, wondering what made him stop when she wanted him to kiss her. And he wanted to do it. It was unfair, teasing her like that. "No, I didn't." She opened her palm. "These were their favorites. When 'Zannah told me the dogs were still here, I brought them with me. And I already visited them in the kennels after my swim."

"You could have warned me."

The dogs sat still, their heads tilted to the side, watching the humans.

"And when would I have the opportunity to do that? You don't come out of that cave of yours unless provoked, and its obvious that no one is welcome in there."

"I'm very busy. And we had dinner together."

"Not by choice, was it?" Phoebe clucked her

tongue and the dogs came to her, parking themselves at her feet. She tossed one biscuit to each and they snatched them out of the air. In seconds, they'd eaten the biscuits and were licking their chops. "They are a little scary."

"Their purpose."

"To keep people out?"

"Yes."

She met his gaze. "I think they're keeping you in, Cain."

His eyes narrowed, defenses rising. "My private life is not your concern."

"What private life? You have no life. You eat, sleep and work, and Mr. Dobbs said you haven't ridden a horse, sailed, even played tennis for ages. For heaven's sake, Cain, you haven't left these grounds in five years."

His eyes darkened, his expression sharpening to lethal. "Leave it alone, Phoebe." He walked away, snapping his fingers. The dogs trotted alongside him.

"Aren't you taking this seclusion too far?"

"I think I'm the best judge of my own life, don't you?"

"I hate seeing you like this."

"Then stay on your side of the house or leave."

"*My* side? You'll have to be more specific, my lord."

He turned, practically snarling at her. "I gave you the east wing, the run of the land, you can go anywhere, do anything you like. Except touch the boats."

"Don't forget except 'bother you.'" She ran after him and grabbed his arm, but he shook her loose. "Cain? Look at me!"

He did, his tone biting as he said, "I'm not your mission, Phoebe. Don't try to make me into something I'm not."

"I wouldn't dream of it."

"Excellent decision." He turned away again, determined to put more than a few yards between them and keep it that way.

"You were a selfish jerk nine years ago and apparently that hasn't changed."

He stopped and turned slowly. He had that whole intimidation thing down pat, Phoebe thought, feeling something close to pain lock inside her.

"You consider a kiss under the staircase a judgment of my character?"

"No, I consider what happened after, a fair assessment of your true self."

"And that would be?"

"Whatever Cain wants, Cain gets."

His expression was menacing for a second, then he looked at the landscape. After a moment, his shoulders drooped a little. "Phoebe," he said gently and met her gaze. "I did not intend to hurt your feelings."

"Yes, you did. You acted like we'd never kissed so I *would* go away."

Cain stared, saying nothing.

"True or not?"

"Yes. It's true."

"I'm fine with that, but what I want to know is, why?"

His gaze zeroed in on her. "Because that kiss made me see that we were incompatible."

She rolled her eyes. "Oh come off it, Blackmon. If we'd gone on for five more minutes and had privacy we'd have been in bed together. How much more compatible do you want?"

"Sex isn't a relationship, Phoebe." He'd had sex with Lily, nothing like his one kiss with Phoebe, but it wasn't enough to make their marriage work. Besides, Phoebe would have never fit into his boardroom lifestyle. She was too unconventional, too outspoken; it would have crushed her.

"I agree, but if you'd given us a chance—oh never mind." She sighed hard. "Forget it. It's past, done, over."

"Apparently not for you."

She lifted her chin, refusing to admit that she'd amused herself with thoughts of what might have been. "I don't believe in lingering in the past that long, Cain. It's a waste of energy. I can't change it, and I won't even try."

Cain wished he could change five years ago. Wished he'd simply divorced Lily instead of trying to make himself love her. She'd ended up hating him anyway. "I apologize for hurting you, Phoebe."

Phoebe frowned, wondering what mystery was hidden behind those tormented eyes of his. "Fine, I accept."

He eyed her. "I'm not convinced."

"Believe what you want. I promise to stay on my side of the house and not trespass in your office or interfere with your life. Or lack thereof."

She spun on her heels, and much to Cain's displeasure, the Dobermans, Jekyll and Hyde, followed her.

Great. His staff, and now his dogs?

He watched her stomp away, every fiber of her body shouting her anger. He didn't blame her. He'd tried to shield her from the man he'd become by staying away from her. He had to. Phoebe made him feel on edge, vulnerable, and if she knew the truth, she'd be gone by morning and never look back.

Even if he couldn't have her, he wanted her near.

On her way to her room, she passed Benson in the hall. He offered her a nightcap, but she declined.

She already knew that liquor would just make her insomnia worse unless she got completely tanked. She wasn't willing to trade a near-death experience with the porcelain god for a couple of hours of sleep. She refused to take sleeping pills, terrified she'd become addicted to the easy way out of her insomnia.

Closing the door behind herself, she glanced around the suite Cain had offered her. With a sitting area that opened to a balcony and a bathroom that would make any woman never want to leave it, it was a perfectly styled antebellum bedroom with only a few modern touches.

A fantasy in pale yellow, blue and lavender, the center was graced with an antique Rice bed, its narrow posts twisting elegantly toward the sky. The heart-shaped palm fronds of the ceiling fan waved a soft breeze on to stir the sheer drapes on the bed.

Crossing the room, she plopped down in the club chair, kicked off her shoes and propped her bare feet on the fat tucked ottoman. Picking up a book she'd been meaning to read for weeks, she opened it and skimmed a few pages. But after a few minutes, even her favorite author couldn't keep her still.

She glanced at her laptop still trapped in its case. It was a glaring reminder that she hadn't written anything worth sending out in weeks. She wasn't hurting for money, but for every five treatments or scripts she did, only one sold. It didn't pay to be a slacker. She wondered how her career would change now that the secret of her pen name had come out. She liked the anonymity of it. She was well aware she wrote weird stuff and didn't want the content to cloud people's judgment of her. Especially producers.

None of her speculation would do her any good if she couldn't come up with a single idea for her next script that was worth the postage.

She pushed out of the chair and went into the bathroom, taking a long, hot shower, pampering herself with a facial and painting her toenails, then slipping into a short chemise, robe and her fluffy slippers with bunny ears on them. The slippers always made her smile, feel silly, and she scuffed along to the French doors, pulling them open. The breeze off the river was warm and balmy, ruffling her hair, her robe.

She sat on the cushioned wicker settee on the balcony, liking that the rail was low enough to offer a view all the way to town. Lights twinkled in the distance, the moonlight glittering like fallen stars on the water. Car headlights riding over the old-bridge flashed like tiny beacons. The scene reminded her that life and excitement weren't far away.

Though she'd had enough of them for a decade.

Phoebe let her mind wander, her imagination coming up with scenarios for the people she couldn't see. She was deep in a scene that was going nowhere when she heard a scuffling sound. Leaving the chair, she leaned out over the rail. The landscape was lit with floodlights in the distance, the large trunks and branches of live oaks looking like gnarled old men ready to capture wayward guests. But she didn't see anyone.

A trickle of fear crept up her spine.

Memories she'd buried surfaced. Kreeg. The strange noises she'd hear around her place and left the comfort of her little house to investigate. Only to find a trail. A rose, a note telling her he was close, but that she was his and would never see him coming.

Instantly she shut off the memories, yet a shiver prickling her skin made her reach for a potted plant, ready to drop it on whomever was lurking below. She heard the sound again, then realized where she was.

Nine Oaks. A near prison, it was so secure.

The dogs were out, she thought, releasing a long breath. They'd bark if there was anyone down there. And Kreeg was behind bars. She was almost tempted to call the police to make certain he hadn't escaped. She set the pot back down, mad at herself for being paranoid. She'd come here to get away from that, dammit. She went inside, closing the doors and climbed into bed.

She would have been surprised that within minutes, she was asleep.

Within ten, she was dreaming.

It was past midnight when Cain headed to bed, and at the top of the staircase, he paused, hearing rapid footsteps and turned. Benson rushed up the stairs behind him, looking pale.

"What's the matter, Benson?"

"It's Miss Phoebe, sir. I heard her. Through the air vents."

"Heard what?"

Then Cain knew. A scream, stifled and long, echoed through the halls.

He waved Benson back and the butler hesitated, then returned to his rooms. Cain hurried into the east wing, knowing exactly where she was, and pushed at the old-fashioned door latch. It was locked. He could hear her whimpering, begging, and threw his shoulder into the door. The latch gave and he rushed inside.

She was on the bed, curled into a tight little ball, hanging onto the bedpost as if it were the mast of a sinking ship. He hurried to the side of the bed, bending over her. Her eyes were tightly shut, her fingers white-knuckled on the post. He called her name, over and over, yet when he touched her, she clawed out at him, catching his cheek and batting at him.

"Phoebe, wake up! It's a dream. Wake up!"

Cain gripped her shoulders, pulling her from the post, and propelled her back on the bed. "Wake up." She fought him. He pressed his weight onto her, stilling her kicking legs and wild punches, then cupped her face. "It's only a dream, honey," he said softly, close to her ear. "Wake up now."

A little sound escaped her, weak and whimpering. Then suddenly, she blinked, staring at him as if he were a stranger, inhaling sharply. Cain felt his insides shift at the confusion in her eyes.

"It's me, Cain. You were dreaming."

Her lip quivered, her chest heaving to bring in needed air, and he eased off her, his hand sliding to her bare shoulder. "It's all right. It was just a dream. No one will hurt you again."

She just stared at him, tears filling her eyes, then she buried her face in his shoulder.

And she cried.

His battle with touching her was outweighed when her fingertips dug into him, and Cain wrapped his arms around her, pulling her into the curve of his body, rubbing her spine. She struggled against her tears, and Cain tightened his arms. He gazed down at her body nestled against his, the supple curves of her leg hitched over his thigh. He wanted to push her onto her back, press himself against her, yet instead, he stroked her spine and bare shoulders, hoping his own body didn't betray him. Her skin was flawless beneath his palm, and she felt so delicate against his roughness. In the silence, he sensed the tension leaving her body, in the way she softened, her curves meshing with his harder planes. Cain could spend a lifetime just like this.

After a moment, she sagged almost bonelessly.

"Sorry," she said sheepishly, and the sound was muffled against his chest.

"How long has this been going on?"

"Weeks."

"What did he do to you?"

"I'd rather not relive it again. I just had the Technicolor version."

He understood and didn't press her, watching her toy with his shirt buttons, wishing she'd yank them open and let him feel her skin against his. "Phoebe?"

"Yeah."

"You okay now?"

She looked up, searching his face. "Yeah. Just peachy." She reached out, sliding her fingers over his jaw, his lips. Cain closed his eyes briefly, smothering a moan as the walls he'd erected started to crumble. He struggled, his mind shouting reasons, flashing pictures that spilled guilt and remorse through him as he caught her hand, stopped her.

He eased back, needing to leave, wanting to stay—and each feeling clawed at him.

Her gaze locked with his. All she did was whisper his name.

Then he was sinking into her mouth.

Nine years of capped electricity connected again.

And exploded.

Four

One touch of her lips and he knew it was madness.

One taste and he was sinking into the abyss of desire.

Cain groaned darkly and gathered her closer.

And the worst happened.

She welcomed him.

Openly, devouring him, letting him taste the sweet energy that was Phoebe. He could easily become an addict. This woman had more power over him than he had over himself. Yet he thirsted for her, sliding his tongue between her lips and indulging in a long-awaited feast.

She arched her body, letting him feel all that she was under the thin cotton, ripe and curved, the plumpness of her breasts burning an imprint into his chest, through layers of cloth. He gripped her slim hips, pulling her to his groin, half crushing her into the downy mattress and still she gave back, bending her knees, wedging him between her thighs.

The heat of her center seared him.

They pawed and stroked, each touch growing more intimate, more desperate for the feel of flesh to flesh. He throbbed for completion, to slide into her body and let the sensations explode between them.

"Cain, oh my," she said against his mouth and opened like a flower again for him. "Nothing's changed, nothing."

Suddenly he jerked back, staring down at her, at the confused frown knitting her smooth forehead.

Everything *had* changed.

He wasn't worthy of this woman. He could not have her as his body demanded and Cain told himself he was stronger than temptation, than his own lust.

"I'm sorry, forgive me."

"Excuse me?"

Cain should have had a clue from her tone that something was about to explode in her as Cain slid back, sitting on the edge of the bed, his head in his hands. "I shouldn't have done that."

"You weren't alone, in case you didn't notice," she said, and he saw she was a little breathless.

Phoebe was very breathless, her body blazing hot, excitement still pouring and pulsing through her although he wasn't touching her. And she needed to be touched by him, only him as she had wanted nearly a decade ago. Yet he was doing the same thing, backing off, running. Even though he was sitting near her feet, he was already gone.

"Leave, Cain. Get out."

He snapped a look at her. It was a mistake. She looked so damn lovely, nestled in the mounds of pillows and embroidered sheets. Her face was flushed and the strap to her top had slid off her shoulder, showing him the roundness of her breasts, teasing him with her rosy beauty.

"You can't do this to me again," she said. "I won't let you."

"Be assured—" he stood "—neither will I."

Phoebe watched him walk to the door, long legs eating up the distance. He grabbed the knob, flinging it open, then went still. "Forgive me," he said without looking at her.

"Stop apologizing! Thanks for bringing me out of the nightmare. Next time, just leave me alone."

Cain felt the knife of her words and didn't blame her. He'd teased her and himself, dangling passion between them, knowing full well it would go no-where the instant his mouth touched hers. He couldn't allow this to develop. Nor would he let her suffer through another nightmare if he could help it. He understood their torment—intimately.

"I'll have the door repaired in the morning." He gestured to the shattered jamb, then simply stepped out and closed the door behind himself.

Cain remained outside, stock-still, his body want-ing her badly while his mind fought to convince it otherwise. He had no right to have anything with Phoebe. Not when the women he *should have* loved was dead because of him.

He headed to his bedroom on the other side of the house, resigned to a night of dreaming of what he could not have and knowing that a dozen rooms separating him from Phoebe truly wouldn't make a difference.

Phoebe felt her eyes water and she stared at the closed door for a long moment, half of her wanting to run and lock it, another part of her wishing he'd turn around and come back in.

And finish what he started.

Damn him. She curled on her side, punching the pillows, still smelling his aftershave on her skin. Did he have to apologize? Twice! *Excuse me, it was good, I liked it, but now I'm really sorry I went all Romeo on you?*

She closed her eyes, wanting sleep, wanting him, and she drew her knees up. It did nothing to alleviate the heavy warmth between her thighs. She couldn't do this again. She couldn't fall for him and not have it returned. Though she'd like to tell herself that his ignoring her hadn't mattered, it had. She was pretty honest with herself, she thought, throwing off the covers and leaving the bed. She'd compared every man to Cain and that first kiss. As if searching for someone who'd give her the same untamed feelings, crackling heat and almost desperate hunger.

A man who'd still want her.

But no other man had compared.

She pushed open the balcony doors, stepping out into the night air. Resting her forearms on the railing, she stared out at the river, the moon's glitter on the water. The fragrance of jasmine and wisteria drifted on the breeze, reminding her of home. She'd grown up in a small town south of Nine Oaks, a dewdrop on back roads where everyone knew who she was and what she'd been up to since grade school. She never got away with anything, she thought with a smile. And oddly, that had made her more mischievous as a kid. She drove her parents crazy, always testing her boundaries, pushing to see what was over the next hill. It was half the reason she went to L.A. when she could have done her writing anywhere.

But here at Nine Oaks, the boundaries were tight, clearly marked. Cain had made that clear from the start. Yet in one instance, she thought, glancing back at the bed, he'd ripped those boundaries apart. Shredded them.

The situation made her see that Cain was a trapped man. Phoebe didn't get to where she was as a writer without doing a lot of people watching and dissecting behaviors. Cain was a surly dragon ensnared in a cave. A beast tormented by something. The memory of his late wife? He must have really loved Lily if her death sent him to this seclusion. But Phoebe had a feeling there was more to it than that. Cain never struck her as a man who did anything he didn't want, and pain and darkness were in his eyes now. He practically oozed with it.

Deciding she wouldn't figure out the mystery tonight, Phoebe turned back into the room, then grabbed a book to read. Sleep wouldn't come for her, she knew. And right now, she was glad.

She didn't want Kreeg invading her dreams again.

Cain sat at his desk, his breakfast tray untouched on the corner. He jotted notes and fielded calls all morning and was starving, but his time was in demand. Working was a good thing since if he had a spare moment, Phoebe leaped into his brain and tormented him.

He hadn't managed the latest crisis when someone rapped on the door.

"Not now, Benson."

The door opened anyway.

"Apparently I wasn't clear enough." Not looking up, Cain scribbled notes.

"Since I'm not Benson that doesn't apply to me, does it?"

Something inside him went still as glass. "People do have to work for a living."

"Yeah sure, whatever."

Finally, he lifted his gaze. He saw the hollowness in her eyes despite how sexy she looked. In curve-hugging cropped jeans and a dainty aqua sleeveless top, she sent the control he'd fought half the night to regain right out the door. "What are you doing in here?"

"Walking, and now sitting down," she said as she did, then set a mug of coffee and a toasted bagel on his desk. She gestured to the breakfast tray. "You haven't eaten?"

"Obviously not. Phoebe, I'm trying to work."

"Take a break. You've been in here since five-thirty this morning."

If she knew that, then she'd been up all night, too, he thought. Had that kiss haunted her as it had him?

"Did you ever get back to sleep?" He sure as hell didn't.

"No, not really." But thinking about him meant that Phoebe wasn't thinking about her own problems. About how she had to testify; how a man she'd dated three times became so obsessed with her that he broke into her car, her house, her bedroom.

She shook the thought loose, focusing on Cain. "Are you going to spend all day in the office?" She folded her legs into the antique chair, looking right at home.

"I normally do."

"Even in the afternoon, evening? Breakfast?" She pushed the plate toward him, then tore off a piece of her bagel and popped it into her mouth.

"Often." Cain snagged a slice of toast from his own tray, biting into it.

"So, you're a recluse in your own house."

"You're on my side of it." He spread jam on the slice, eating that, then picking up his fork and attacking the still-warm eggs.

"Is there a line?" She looked around at the beautifully carpeted floor. "Be specific, Cain. I thought I had the run of the place."

"You do."

She simply arched a brow, the bagel poised for a bite. "But not here. In this room." She munched.

"I like my privacy to work and you have an entire wing for yourself."

She waved as she chewed and swallowed. "Yeah, but the fun stuff happens on your side."

Cain couldn't help but smile. "I hadn't noticed."

"You don't notice much at all, do you?" She finished off her bagel, then sipped her decaf coffee.

You, he thought, I notice you in every way. Then he said, "Sure I do, I run the place."

She rolled her eyes. "Ha. Benson runs this house, you run your companies, and I'm betting that they won't fall apart with one day's inattention."

"On the contrary, my world will crash." To make his point, the phone rang. He answered it, asking the caller to hold, then looked at her.

Phoebe sensed he was grateful for the call and stood. "Live for the moment, Cain. Hang up."

"I can't."

"Well, I'm going for a ride. Want to come with me?"

"On a horse?"

"Unless you have something else to ride." Instantly Phoebe wished the words back and tried not to blush. "Yes, a horse. Gallop, canter. You know, the four-legged things out there in the stables?"

"No, thank you."

"Fine, be the king reigning over the fiefdom. But you owe me a dinner." She headed to the door.

"I do?"

"Yes, and I'll nag you till you join me like a civilized person."

Cain pushed the hold button on the call and went after her. "Phoebe, I'd rather not—"

"I'm not listening," she said in a singsong voice, walking toward the front door. She passed Benson saying, "Two for dinner, Benson, make sure he shows up," then cast a sexy glance at him that rocked him to his heels before she disappeared out the front door.

Cain stared at the closed door, then looked at Benson standing at the base of the stairs.

"Persistent young lady," was all the butler said and marched up the stairs.

"She's a damn pest."

"Of course, sir."

"Well, she is," he muttered to himself and turned back to the library. He refused to turn on the cameras on his screens and watch her. He'd let security take care of it instead. If he began checking on her, he'd turn into a crazed voyeur and what did that say about him?

He suddenly felt like the Hunchback of Notre Dame, watching the world from afar and wishing for more.

Just as he considered joining her, his gaze landed on the picture of his late wife. Guilt set in instantly, reminding him that he'd ruined her life because he couldn't love her. He lusted after Phoebe and even if that were satisfied, he'd ruin her, too. He smacked the photo facedown on the desk.

Yet an hour later, he was walking through the house toward the rear, stepping out on the veranda in time to see Phoebe gallop across the lawn at full speed on his finest mare. Given her personality, he would have expected her to take the stallion, but Mr. Dobbs had more sense than to let her ride the mean-spirited horse.

She threw her arms out wide, letting go of the reins and riding the chestnut horse with the strength of her knees. He watched her, her laughter pinging through the warm air and sliding over Cain like a cloak. It had been a very long time since a woman had laughed in this house, he thought, then turned away from the sight of her.

For Cain, the temptation of Phoebe DeLongpree was more than he could handle.

Cajun music was rocking the kitchen as Phoebe swept the mop over the kitchen floor. Willis was at the long worktable, polishing silver that didn't need polishing while a male servant ironed napkins and a tablecloth at the other end. She was here because she was already tired of being alone to amuse herself, and Willis was a fun person to be around. He joked easily as he did his work, which in her opinion was busywork. Without guests in the house and few to cook for and look after, the servants were as bored as she was.

Jean Claude was singing along, sounding rather good as he punched dough for bread.

"Willis, lift your feet."

"Oh yeah sure, like there is an inch that you didn't already get, Miss Phoebe?"

"Do a job well and you won't have to do it twice."

"How much caffeine have you had this morning, *bébé*?" Jean Claude said, chuckling as she rinsed the mop and attacked the floor again.

Before she could answer, a deep voice cut through the noise like the crack of lightning. "What the hell are you doing?"

Phoebe whipped around. Cain loomed in the doorway, and the room instantly quieted. Jean Claude shut off the radio.

Oh hell. He looks furious, she thought, not willing to bow to his bluster. "You're smart, figure it out," she said and heard several indrawn breaths.

"You're mopping the floor?" he said, louder than necessary.

"See, I knew you were smart."

"Put that mop down and let the servants do their jobs, Phoebe."

Phoebe glanced around at the stoic faces, then leaned the mop against the counter and marched right up to Cain. "Excuse me?"

"I said—"

"I heard you. Are you giving me orders, Cain Blackmon?"

"I'm warning you not to bother my employees in their jobs."

"Or else? Or you'll what? Toss me out? Be grouchier than you already are?" She poked at his chest as she spoke. "Well, let me tell you, Augustus Cain Blackmon the fourth, I don't take kindly to you growling at me." The more she poked, the farther Cain stepped back out of the kitchen. "You can hand that ogre-in-the-castle stuff to everyone else, but not me. Got that?"

"You're interfering with the workings of this house!"

"Really, show me then?" She gestured around herself. "There is nothing to do. You don't use most of the house. The flowers are in bloom in the solarium, did you know that? The furniture in there still has the packaging from the store on it. Heck, there's enough groceries in that kitchen to feed a battalion of Marines, and enough rooms in here to house them all. But it's just you, Cain, no one else. It's a waste. All these people around for *your* beck and call? Honestly, fend for yourself once and—"

"And you're changing the subject," he butted in.

She looked away, then back and muttered, "Yeah well, it seemed like a good idea at the time."

Cain stared down at her, liking the spark of anger in her eyes. She wasn't the least bit intimidated by him when most people ran for cover. Part of him wondered if he was just looking for an excuse to growl when she was having a good time with the servants because Lily barely spoke to them except to give orders. Comparing the women made him angry again, and as if she could tell, she backed up.

"Regardless of what is used or wasted, it's my decision and I'm asking you to leave them to their jobs."

"No."

His eyes narrowed. "I beg your pardon?"

Hers narrowed right back. "They're my friends and I won't stop speaking to them because you demand it. And because they are all working like nuts for you, the only time I can is while they are at their jobs. So no. I won't leave them be."

Cain gritted his teeth, wanting to shake her. Or kiss her.

And when she spoke, her voice was lower, softer. "Your staff are grateful for the jobs, but I don't think they like you very much. Do you want to live like that? Intimidating everyone?"

No, he didn't. It was five years of loneliness that made him feel so on edge. Or was it just that she was near, tempting him? "Except you?"

"I don't have a stake in ticking you off. They do." She gazed up into his dark eyes. "Life would be more pleasant around here if you didn't snap at everyone. These people practically fear you!"

He arched a brow, a look that said it wasn't a concern.

Her gaze thinned.

Cain felt inspected and found lacking.

"I don't like you right now."

"Really?"

"No, not at all." She marched back into the kitchen, apologizing to the staff for *his* behavior, then walked past him without a glance and down the long hall.

"Phoebe," he called.

She just put her hand up behind her head, waved him off and kept going. When she was out of sight, Cain stared at the floor, his polished shoes, the pristine floor, then lifted his gaze to the immaculate house—not a speck of dust, not a thing out of its precise place.

He almost, in that moment, wished for messy, for lived-in, for the sound of voices and laughter he'd heard just moments ago. She was right, it was as if no one lived here. Like a museum of fine things no one appreciated. Or used.

Cain pushed his fingers through his hair and let out a long-suffering sigh. He stepped into the kitchen, apologized, then went to his office, suddenly hating the four walls and himself.

That evening, Cain sat at the table in the formal dining room, waiting.

She didn't arrive.

But Benson did.

"Well? She demanded this meal with me, where is she?"

Benson cleared his throat uncomfortably. "Miss Phoebe has decided to dine in her room, sir."

Cain hated the pity in Benson's eyes, though he'd never let it show in his face.

"She did have a message for you."

"I'll bet. Well, what is it?"

"She agrees to stay on her side of the house, sir. With pleasure."

Cain's features pulled taut. He stood, leaving the aromatic meal behind and headed back to his office.

He didn't make it, glancing up the staircase and shaking his head. The woman wasn't even around and she was turning him inside out.

"Shall I bring your dinner into the office, sir," Benson said.

"No, thank you."

Cain started to walk away, then said, "Wait, I'll take that." Cain gathered the plate, napkin and utensils from the tray Benson held.

"Sir?"

"Go relax, Benson. Take a break." The butler's brows shot up. "I'm fine," Cain assured him, suddenly realizing that he let Benson cater to him and had gotten too used to the fact. But then, Benson was his only company.

Cain walked to the solarium, stepped inside, then set the plate down before he stripped the plastic off the new furniture.

He sat at the little bistro table in the corner, his feet propped on another chair, eating alone, staring at the abundance of color bursting in the sunny room. The paddle fan overhead moved the sweet fragrances around him.

This was his mother's favorite room. She swore to all, she'd married his father just so she could enjoy it. And halfway through his dinner, Cain faced the fact that Phoebe was right. Damn it. He hadn't enjoyed his own house. Even after he'd spent a fortune restoring it.

Good God. There would be no living with her now. That was *if* she decided to speak with him again.

Five

Cain pulled at the sash to his robe and paused at the top of the staircase, looking toward the opposite wing, knowing Phoebe was there somewhere down that long hall.

He hadn't seen her in two days. Good to her word, she'd kept to the east wing. Once in awhile he'd hear her voice, drawn by it, but when he looked, she was gone, off doing God knew what, far from him.

She was like a mystical being, darting off into the forest when the evil human came near.

It made his isolation feel more pronounced than it was before she arrived. It shouldn't matter, he told himself, but he didn't like knowing that she was mad at him.

Nor did he like how he'd treated her. He wanted to apologize, but seeking her was out of the question. Alone with Phoebe was not a good thing.

Especially at night.

He descended the stairs, intent on the kitchen and something to quiet the growling in his stomach and perhaps make him sleep. Her insomnia was catching, he thought. He knew of it because Benson reported that she prowled the house at odd hours or that the lights were on in her suite nearly constantly.

Cain wondered if he was here because he hoped to run into her. And what kept her from sleeping? Her attacker was in jail, and the trial was set for a couple of weeks from now. Was she still afraid? She'd nothing to fear here at Nine Oaks, that was for certain.

He stepped into the kitchen, reaching for the switch when he saw a figure sitting on the worktable. The light over the range glowed enough for him to recognize her. She looked over her shoulder toward him, but he couldn't see her face. Then she turned away quickly and Cain could swear she was wiping at her eyes.

"Phoebe, are you okay?"

If okay meant being woken by nightmares,

Phoebe thought. She was actually relieved he'd interrupted her. The pity party was getting really pathetic. "Sure I am. Come in, I won't bite."

"Just as well, I'm in no mood to battle."

"Like that would matter to me?"

Cain smirked to himself and moved into the kitchen, flipping on another light.

She immediately closed her robe a little tighter, suddenly aware they were both in pajamas.

He looked at her snack selection. "Ice cream? At this hour?"

"Anytime is good for Rocky Road." She shoved a scoop into her mouth and smiled hugely.

He sensed it was forced, noticing the redness in her eyes, but he didn't pry. He opened the refrigerator, staring into it, then gathered the makings of a sandwich and set it on the worktable near her. He went for bread and a cutting board and then started slicing.

"Benson said you've been up late a lot. Do you even try to sleep?" he asked.

She dug into the tub of ice cream. "Sure. Count sheep, imagine a white room, clear my thoughts with meditation. Nothing works. Drugs are just too easy to get dependent on."

"You keep thinking of him, don't you?"

Her head snapped up, her expression sharp.

"Yeah, some." She deflated, like a barrier sliding away. "Rational thought tells me he's locked up, but I can't help the feeling that—" her shoulders moved restlessly "—that he's behind me, watching."

"He isn't."

"But he's rich enough to get out on bail, Cain. His lawyers have already smeared my reputation and warned me that I couldn't put him away." She clamped her lips shut, fighting the wave of fear that came.

"He will go to jail." Cain sliced roast beef, waiting till she gathered her composure, though his arms ached to comfort her. "What did he do to you?"

She hopped off the table and put the ice cream back in the freezer. "He taunted me," she said carelessly, but Cain heard the fear still lingering in her tone. "I don't want to talk about it."

"Fine. Sandwich?"

She shook her head, but snatched a slice of meat anyway.

Cain was surprised she didn't rush off, but stayed near, watching him, then lifted her gaze to his face. He didn't have to make eye contact to know it. He could feel it on his skin. It raised the tension in the large room, narrowing the space around them. He felt charged, crackling with her energy. Cain could smell her perfume, sense the cloth lying against her skin, the soundless slide of silk. And the memory of kissing her so wildly poured through his brain and doused his body with desire.

He swallowed hard and lifted his gaze to hers. "I'm sorry, Phoebe."

"Since we exchanged some nasty words, I'll ask for what?"

"For all of it, for the way I spoke to you, treated you the other day."

She met his gaze. "I forgive you."

His brow shot up.

She smiled. "I'm not as hard-nosed as you think, Cain. Don't give me orders again, though."

"I should have remembered that you never did like restrictions."

"That's from a childhood of everyone knowing what I was up to and squealing to my parents. Which got me grounded and watched even harder."

"I know the feeling. I had a houseful of people that knew what I was up to constantly."

"Yeah, but you were the boss."

"Not always."

She rolled her eyes. "Get real. Might as well have been. No one is going to stop the prince of Nine Oaks from doing what he wants."

He spread mayo on the bread and slapped together a sandwich. "Are you saying I'm spoiled?"

Phoebe fetched him a plate. "Yes, of course you are."

He didn't use it, cutting the sandwich and eating it off the table. "Good God, you are blunt. Why do I feel a lecture coming?" he said, then bit into the sandwich.

She nipped a pickle from the pile he'd sliced. "Want one? I hate being lectured. But now that you asked..."

He swallowed fast to defend himself. "I didn't."

"Coward."

That brow shot up, looking more darling to her than menacing. She didn't think he'd want to hear that observation. "You're used to everyone jumping to your tune."

Except her. She danced to her own music. He liked that about her, but felt the need to put in his two cents. "How about you? You want everyone to be on the same tempo—*yours*. Which is high-octane and in fast-forward."

"True," she admitted, shocking him. She started putting away the food. "But life is too short to waste it on anything, except doing what you want."

"But you're not doing what you want. You're here, hiding out."

"From the press and phone calls. And hello? Don't throw stones, Blackmon. Why have you refused to leave this place in five years?"

Instantly his mood changed. Phoebe felt it as if a

door slammed somewhere. His body tensed, eyes shuttered. "Don't dissect me."

Slowly she set down a jar and inched closer, forcing him to look at her. He was so darkly handsome, she thought, dressed in rich satins, looking very powerful and wealthy. And incredibly sad.

"You opened this subject, Cain."

Her voice was so gentle Cain felt an ache burst in his chest. He set the last half of the sandwich down, pushing away the plate. "I'm sorry I did."

"You loved her that much?"

His head snapped up, his gaze sharp and suddenly icy.

"Your wife, Lily. She must have been a wonderful person."

"Is that what you think? That I'm mourning her?" Oh for pity sake, Cain thought. The rest of the world thought that, but he didn't want Phoebe believing the lie. Yet he wouldn't tell her the truth, either.

"Well, yes…no, I mean, my mind doesn't sit still so I can think of all sorts of reasons, but Suzannah believes—"

"Suzannah hasn't a clue."

"Because you won't confide in her."

"She doesn't need to know and neither do you."

She reared back for a second, hurt by the razor bite in his tone. For a moment, he looked so tortured and ashamed that she knew she had to be misreading the look.

"Cain? Look at me."

He didn't, closing jars and wrapping food instead. "Don't think I'm so noble, Phoebe. You'll be sorely disappointed."

He strode out abruptly, leaving her feeling suddenly cold and unprotected. She stared at the empty doorway for a moment, then finished cleaning up the mess. She stopped to eat the untouched half of his sandwich and as she munched, one thing stuck in her thoughts: he wasn't mourning Lily. So why on earth was he torturing himself with hiding away here?

"Don't look at me like that, Benson," Phoebe said. "He'll do it."

Benson's stoic expression spoke his doubt. "I wish only to spare you heartache, Miss Phoebe." The butler handed her the picnic basket and draped the blanket over her arm. "He will not join you."

"Doesn't hurt to try, does it?"

Phoebe understood his concern and she was touched, since a wiser, more sensible part of herself agreed with him, and warned her to leave Cain alone, mind her own business and enjoy the estate.

Yet another part of her ached for the man he'd become. The one she saw last night. Gone were the easy smiles, the charm from years ago. Though his mere presence still set her heart pounding and her body—well…on fire, it was her soul that cried for him.

Like I've known him for centuries, she thought again.

She ignored the fact that by focusing on him she didn't have time to think about Kreeg and his band of lawyers and what else she'd lose. Those problems seemed so trivial right now. The wiser part of her lost. Easily.

It was her nature to interfere.

Especially when Benson told her that although they'd argued, Cain waited for her in the dining room to join her for dinner. As far as she was concerned, she owed him a meal.

She walked briskly out the front door, then around the west wing toward the veranda outside the library. The best way to get him to come with her would be to coax him out on this beautiful day. Which he could see from his cave.

Tempt him with food, she thought, and rapped on the glass door, waiting, her stomach in knots.

Cain left his chair, frowning and wondering who the hell was disturbing him from the patio. When he flung open the door, he was struck first by how beautiful she was in the afternoon light, the sun gleaming off her hair blowing in the breeze, the bright smile she offered despite how he'd snapped at her last night. When he finally dragged his gaze from her compact body in shorts and a simple T-shirt, and those incredible legs, he saw the basket on her arm.

"No."

Her smile melted, and he hated himself for it.

"But you haven't heard my proposition."

"It's rather obvious, Phoebe."

"Aren't you hungry? Wouldn't you like a break from that dark dismal room with all those computers and phone calls and people bugging you?"

"Does that include you?"

"Of course not," she said with an easy smile. If she had to use force, she would, and she grabbed his arm, pulling him toward her and out into the sun. He actually squinted against the brightness, and Phoebe knew she was doing the right thing.

"It's gorgeous, breezy and just look at the million-dollar view." She gestured to the flowers blooming, the live oaks elegantly festooned with Spanish moss. "Come on. Play with me."

The implication shot through him like a crack of lightning, and Cain stiffened. Her look dared him, invited him. Hell. He wanted to do much more than play with her. And he couldn't. Not with Phoebe. He'd be consumed whole if he let himself indulge in her, even if she was only suggesting a picnic. God help him, he didn't want to hurt this woman. And he knew, eventually, he would.

"Phoebe, I know you mean well and you think you're trying to help, but I do not want it."

"Help with what?"

"Me. My life."

She gave him a long look up and down that ignited his blood, then said, "You're a grown man, and don't need my help. Whatever reasons that you've made yourself a recluse, it's your business. I'm bored and while I enjoy my own company, I want to have a picnic and I'd love for you to join me."

"You aren't giving up on this, are you?"

"Nope. Face it. I'll be a nuisance."

She got behind him, giving him a push, and Cain smiled when he didn't move. She kept trying like a kid who wanted someone to ride the roller coaster with her and could find no takers.

"I have work to do."

"You're the boss, take a day off. And if you say your company can't stand the inattention, then you're not that good at running it."

He twisted to look at her. "That's a gauntlet you've thrown down, m'lady."

"Then pick it up, m'lord." She winked. "Take the challenge."

Cain wanted to go, he truly did. Spending a couple of hours with her was like drinking in sunshine. And she was her usual energetic and impatient self. It was addicting.

"All right, but let me change."

"Oh no," she said, pushing him toward the stone path. "It's a 'Come as you are' party. You're not getting a chance to talk yourself out of this."

"God, you're an imp." And a delight, he thought.

"So what else is new?" She flashed him that smile, and Cain felt a renewing feeling race through him when he saw it.

He took the basket from her. "Good grief, what's in here?"

"Jean Claude's Cajun fried chicken…"

"For an army?"

"Oh, there's more, but it's a surprise." They walked toward the shore.

Cain felt apprehension creep up his spine. He hadn't been near the water in a long time.

"Want to take a boat ride?"

"No." And he didn't want her to take one, either.

"Okay, fine. The docks then."

"I'd rather not."

"Be brave, I'll protect you," she said, already walking briskly toward the pier.

Cain watched her go, his hands on his hips. The

woman was rather comfortable with her own stubbornness. She headed toward the open-air gazebo at the end of one dock. It was more of a place to sit and relax while watching the movement on the river than to dock the boats. Cain hadn't been here in five years.

As thoughts of Lily and her death started to crowd his mind, Cain shook them loose and started walking.

When he caught the scent of the bug fogger and noticed the area was swept clean of debris, he realized she had a conspirator. Yet instead of sitting in the loungers, she went right to the edge of the pier, spread out the blanket and relaxed.

Phoebe glanced over her shoulder, wondering why he looked so apprehensive just then. "Come, sit." She patted the space near her, and when he set the basket down, she opened it.

Cain realized this would be an old-fashioned picnic in more ways than just sitting on the docks with a pretty girl when she lifted out bowls and plates wrapped in cloth and tied with ribbon.

He was touched beyond measure. She'd planned this carefully, so determined that he join her. He felt honored. He took off his shoes and socks, and her gaze followed him as he lowered himself to the decking.

"See. That wasn't so hard, was it?"

"Painful. I have ugly feet."

She glanced. "You have big feet," she teased, her eyes twinkling as she dipped her foot in the water, swishing while she unwrapped food and served up two plates.

"There's something about eating outside that makes you take your time, enjoy the view and the tastes."

"Are you making excuses for bullying me?"

"Bullying you? Ha." She poured sweet raspberry iced tea into thick glasses and handed him one. "You needed to get out or you would have barked and growled and crawled back into your cave."

"I think I resent that description."

Her gaze sparked with a challenge. "Deny it, I dare you."

His lips curved as he met her gaze over the rim of the glass. "Never. You'd gloat." He sipped once, then bit into a chicken leg and moaned at the explosion of flavors.

"See, wasn't it worth Jean Claude's talent?"

He merely nodded, hungrier than he'd thought as he finished off the chicken and reached for something else to try. Then suddenly he fingered the edge of the quilt, smiling to himself. "My grandmother's mother made this."

She looked startled at the red, white and blue

quilt. "Oh no. Maybe we shouldn't use it. Benson gave it to me."

He waved that off. "No, no, she always said things were made to be used and not viewed from afar."

"Sounds like my mom. There wasn't much in our house that didn't have a practical use."

He stared out over the water. "I used to love sitting out here when I was a kid, fishing and never catching a thing. Just thinking."

"Alone time. I do that a lot."

"I watched one of your movies."

She looked up, chewing. "Really? I just write the stories. Once I sell them, I don't have any more to say about who plays the roles or what the directors change. I've only been hired to do the on-site writes once."

"Just the same, you have an amazing talent."

She blushed.

"And a twisted mind."

"Rest assured, it's all fictitious."

"Good, you had me worried."

She smiled and nipped a spoonful of shrimp salad. "I would be huge if I ate like this all the time. Jean Claude has my undying love and admiration."

"Can't cook?"

"Sure I can. Open the package, set the timer, nuke it." He chuckled and his smile changed his whole appearance, Phoebe thought. Now that's the man she remembered.

"Even I have more talent than that."

"Some people are good at some things, some at others. I don't cook." She glanced up as she said, "Only because I never really had to do it, but I'm more than willing to pay those with the talent for their wares." She shrugged as if that made perfect sense and dug into the fruit compote and sweet cream.

"I went into the solarium," he said suddenly.

She met his gaze. "Oh yeah?"

She licked cream off her upper lip, and he was enthralled with her tongue passing over that lush mouth. "You were right, there are a lot of rooms no one uses, least of all me."

"It's lovely in there. I think it's my favorite room."

"Have you ever seen the whole house?"

She rolled her eyes, lifting a spoon of shrimp salad for him. "You should taste this."

He caught her hand and brought it to his mouth. He ate off her spoon and something shattered between them, a barrier, a wall, he didn't know what. "So have you seen the whole plantation?"

He was closer now, close enough that she could see the sparkle of gold in his eyes. Sexy, restrained power.

"Yeah, except your bedroom."

"That can be arranged," he said in a heavy voice.

Awareness simmered between them. "Is that an invitation?" She arched a tapered brow.

His body clenched at the thought. "For a tour," he clarified wisely, yet the image of her in his bed sent his mind off to a place he shouldn't go.

"Oh, well. How about showing me all of the secret passages?"

"'Zannah told you," he muttered dryly, then dipped his spoon into her shrimp salad. "When?"

"Years ago," she said with feeling. "How do you think we skipped out of here so often?"

He shrugged. "Conning Benson."

"I adore him, but no. He'd tell if we'd really misbehaved."

He was eating off her plate, she off his, tasting and sharing, so that neither realized the time passing. For long moments, Cain listened to her chat about her family. Phoebe had a sister and brother, both married with children and living on another coast. Cain's parents were off on a summer tour of Europe.

"I'd have thought you'd be married with kids by now, Phoebe."

She groaned. "You sound like my mother."

He made a rolling motion for her to keep going.

"Yes, I want all those girlie dreams, marriage, kids…someday I'll have a house full of children."

She got a faraway look that pricked his heart. "You certainly have the energy to chase after them."

She smiled. "They're such fun. Everything is new to them. Makes you look at the world differently. I think people make the mistake of thinking that once they can talk, they can also understand."

Cain drew up his knee and leaned his back against the post. He wasn't interested in eating or the view, but in listening to her, watching her. She sat with one leg bent, the other swinging slowly in the water as she hovered over the meal. Her appetite was nothing short of startling for one so small. Her petite size made him feel so gargantuan near her. Protective.

Thoughts of Kreeg and what he might have done to her crept into his mind, and he bit back the questions that plagued him. He didn't want to ruin this peaceful moment with her. He was deep in his own thoughts and didn't notice she was standing till she brushed him. He looked up.

"I want to move this back from the sun," she said, and he stood to help her tug the quilt farther under the shade.

She was on the edge, reaching for his tea glass when Cain twisted to take it from her. She turned at the same time, and he bumped her.

He heard her indrawn breath and stared, horrified

as she lost her footing, then dropped backward into the water.

"Phoebe!" He scrambled to the edge, kneeling, impatient for her to surface. "Phoebe!" Oh God. He drove his hand under the water and felt nothing. Memories of Lily crowded rational thought, his heartbeat escalating out of control.

Phoebe popped up, pushing her hair out of her face and laughing hysterically. "Oh, for pity sake."

"Give me your hand!" He reached out.

"It's okay." She treaded water. "I'm fine." She dived under, then came up closer to him. Instantly, he scooped her under the arms and lifted her out of the water and onto the dock. Then she was in his arms, his strength crushing her to his body. He buried his face in the curve of her neck, his breathing fast and harsh.

Something's very wrong, Phoebe thought. "You're getting wet."

"I don't care."

Then she realized he was trembling. She eased back to look at him, and brushed his hair off his face, cupped his lean jaw. Then she remembered his wife had died from drowning.

"Cain, talk to me. I was on a swim team, remember? You don't have to worry."

But he was in another place, in darkness and pain

and guilt. She could see it in his eyes, in the way his gaze scraped over her features.

"Phoebe," he whispered, passing his hand over her wet hair. Then smoothly he lowered his head, his mouth capturing hers, fusing her with the mind-blowing heat that always bubbled between them.

It needed only a spark to make it flame, she thought.

And this was it.

Six

If passion had a sound, it was a deep ripping tear. If it could be seen, it was hissing steam vented between them, sliding and pouring over her.

Her feet left the ground as he stepped back from the edge. But that didn't stop his consuming kiss, the power grinding through her with nearly painful clarity. She could barely draw a breath his embrace was so tight, his hands fisting in her wet clothes as if to drive her into him.

She felt gloriously smothered and devoured and wanted.

And she let go. Of her emotions, her desire. His

body hardened against her, thrilling her, and her hands climbed up his chest, wrapping his neck.

Cain groaned and kept kissing, unwilling to break it off, unwilling to give in to the denial in his mind. His hands charged a wild ride over her body, and as if he couldn't stand on his own power, he fell back against the support post.

Phoebe went with him, wedged to him and when he cupped her breast, she thought she'd disintegrate. When he thumbed her nipple, she knew she would.

She pushed into his touch, letting him know it was okay, that she wanted him, too. Yet she could feel something inside him battling with his need. She hoped he fought it. He broke the kiss only to draw in more air, then devoured her mouth again, moaning deeply when her hands shaped the contours of his chest, and lower.

She was bold and provocative, and Cain hungered for it, for the womanly sounds, for the feel of her flesh melting with his. He wanted her now, right now, and he tore his mouth from hers, but couldn't stop as he nibbled her jaw, her throat.

"Phoebe, you make me crazy."

"Oh yeah, same here," she whispered, sliding her hand down and letting her fingers slip over his erection.

The sound he made was part pain and part pleasure and she wanted to be naked and warm with him, wanted the freedom to experience, and explore what had haunted her for years.

He leaned his head back, his lungs laboring. "I'm a basket case around you," he said, and the hint of regret made her touch his jaw and force him to meet her gaze.

"Don't you dare apologize." She nipped at his mouth.

"I wasn't planning on it."

She searched his handsome face for a moment. "You were scared."

His features tightened. "Out of my mind."

"I can swim, Cain, rather well. I'll show you the awards for it, if you want?"

His lips quirked. "Not necessary."

"I like that you were, though."

"Say again?"

"Not because of Lily, but that you cared enough."

"Oh man, Phoebe. Don't you get it? I want you like breathing."

"And then what?"

"Huh?"

"After having me, then what?"

He said nothing, and she could see the openness she'd just shared with him dissolve a little.

She stepped back out of his arms, her body still tingling, still hungering. "I see."

"Phoebe." He tried to grab her back.

"I'm a fantasy, I get it. That's okay. I've never been the fantasy of a recluse before."

He didn't think she was okay with it at all, or she wouldn't be miffed, and part of him was screaming for joy over it. Yet reality had a way of crashing in and he said, "Yes, I am a recluse, but now, so are you." He caught her by the arms, turning so her back was to the gazebo railing.

She frowned up at him. "What are you doing?"

"Look beyond me, near the fence line."

She peered around him, to the woods separating the land from the road and saw a white news van.

"We both have good reasons."

There were photographers in there, she knew. And he was shielding her.

"Oh no." Her gaze snapped to his. "Do you think they photographed us?"

"If they have a long-range lens, yes. Probably."

"Great." Her shoulders drooped.

"Ashamed?"

"No. You?" He shook his head, his gaze intense and scrutinizing. "I'm thinking of what the press will do with more pictures. It could hurt you."

Though he didn't care what happened to him, he was moved by the thought. "They've been using me for fodder for years, Phoebe, I don't care."

"But you knew they were there?"

"They've pretty much camped out there since you drove through the gates."

"I'll have to remember that." She glanced at him under a lock of deep red hair, smiling devilishly. If those idiots weren't in the van, she'd have stripped for Cain and played with him right here, right now.

As if he could understand her thoughts, his expression grew darker, his eyes smoky-brown and sultry. She glanced to the left toward the van they could barely see. Then she ducked low. When he stared down at her frowning, she pulled him to the deck.

"I say we hide from them." She started stuffing the picnic lunch back in the basket.

"I beg your pardon?"

"Let's run. We'll see if they are really watching."

"Phoebe, we don't have to. Who cares what they want?"

"I know." She looked up and the delightful gleam in her eyes caught him in the heart. "It's the principle of it."

She was daring him and Cain felt as if he hovered on the edge of fun. He wanted badly to jump in. "Leave that," he said suddenly, taking her hand and pulling her from the dock. "We can get it later." He looked toward the property line and could see figures moving toward a break in the trees. "Run."

Phoebe didn't have to be told twice and barefoot and wet they took off down the dock. Cain's legs were twice as long, and Phoebe tried to keep up as they raced across the lawn toward the east of the house. The mansion was on a small jut in the land, and they hurried across the curve toward the rear where the pool and stables were located.

She couldn't keep up. "Cain," she said and he paused, glanced, then scooped her up, darting around the edge of the house, then flattening against the wall. She laughed as he lowered her feet to the ground. He kept her close as he peered around the edge.

"The little fools are moving. I'm betting they'll try to get near the east orchard." He shifted back and grinned down at her.

Her breath caught hard.

Everything around her faded at the sight of his handsome face lit up with delight. Her throat tightened and she smiled back, absorbing it. What woman could resist this man when he smiled like that?

A few yards from them, a groundskeeper paused in pruning bushes, and started moving toward them. "Mr. Blackmon, you all right, sir?"

"Fine ah…"

"Mark," Phoebe supplied softly.

"We're fine, Mark. Thanks."

The man nodded, not convinced, yet went back to work.

Cain looked down at her, surprised. "You knew his name?"

"Yeah, *I* pay attention." She nudged him.

Overhead the sky darkened, rain threatening and she looked up. "Oh no, the quilt!"

"It's been left in the rain before and it's under the gazebo." He looked around the edge of the wall again.

"Think we lost them?"

"Don't count on it. I suspect the instant they knew I had a houseguest, they beefed up their spying techniques." He gestured toward the house and they started walking.

"Sorry about that."

"I'm used to it."

"I'm not."

"From what I've read, they haven't been kind to you."

Her expression saddened. "They've single-handedly destroyed my reputation, too."

"I think you'll be more in demand, especially when Kreeg is behind bars for good."

"I doubt it. He's got money and power and that makes people do what the rest of us can't."

He heard a bit of chastising in her tone but let it go. "Such as?"

"Making certain their side of the story is told and not the real one."

"I know he's lying, Phoebe."

"So do I, but the jurors might not, and might think I'm nothing but a gold digger or something."

"What does your lawyer think?"

"That he might get off with a slap on the wrist and a restraining order."

No wonder she was scared he'd come after her. "Then you need a new lawyer."

"I can barely afford the one I have."

"We'll see about that."

She stopped walking, and droplets of rain pelted her upturned face. "What do you mean?"

"I'll make certain you have the best."

"No."

He scowled. "Why not?"

"I don't want charity and I don't want you dragged into this. It's bad enough that I have to hide in the first place, but I won't have your name dragged in the mud with mine."

Cain's gaze sketched her features, his expression hardening. "Do you want him to pay for his crime?"

"Of course."

"Then you have to fight fire with fire. Not with a match."

She opened her mouth to object and Cain gathered

her in his arms, the rain coming harder now. "Let me do this. I can and I want to." He needed to protect her from Kreeg. Or maybe from himself. She was alone in her battle and she didn't need to be.

"Please, Phoebe, I have the resources."

Phoebe nodded finally and Cain pressed his lips to her forehead. The clouds unleashed and they stood there in each other's arms, feeling something weave around them and bind them. Fear eased, loneliness receded.

Cain wondered how he'd handle those feelings when they came back. When she was gone.

Yet all Phoebe knew was, for now, she had a true champion.

Several moments later, Benson appeared at their side, holding an umbrella. "I beg your pardon, sir, but did you by chance notice it was raining?"

They looked at him, then at each other and laughed.

"Really?" Cain said and, dismissing the offer of the umbrella, they headed toward the house. The rain fell suddenly harder, lightning cracking overhead, and they ran, ducking inside.

Cain shook his head like a dog, then looked at her. She was plucking at her shirt molded to her body and showing him the shape and curves beneath. In a flour sack, she'd still be sexy as hell, he thought. A servant showed up with towels, and handed them each one.

Cain toweled her hair, then wrapped her in the terry cloth blanket.

"You'll catch a cold."

"I have a great immune system."

"Go change before Benson goes all nursemaid on you."

Benson made a face as if that behavior was beyond him.

She nodded and started to walk away, then turned, walking backward. "Cain."

He glanced up from rubbing the towel over his hair. "Yes?"

"Sometimes you surprise me."

He smiled gently. "You always surprise me, Phoebe."

She turned away, heading to her room, leaving wet footprints on the wood floor.

Cain looked at Benson, smiling sheepishly, then told him they left the picnic at the gazebo. But Benson simply stared, looking a little stunned.

"What's the matter?" Cain asked.

"It's been years since I've seen you smile, sir."

His expression fell a little and Cain glanced to where Phoebe had disappeared. "Yes, I know. Get it while it lasts." Because when she learns the truth, she'll be gone.

Cain had a taste of what life would be like with her and the bittersweet knowledge that he'd never have more was slowly killing him inside.

An hour later, Cain was in the library, shaking things up. First, he'd called Phoebe's lawyer and wasn't impressed. The man was either not good enough to represent her side or was simply too inexperienced to handle Kreeg's fleet of attorneys.

So Cain called his own, who enlisted the best criminal lawyer in the state. After half an hour on the phone, he was satisfied that Phoebe was represented fairly. He called his broker next.

"Sell all of my Kreeg CGI stock."

"I wouldn't advise that, Mr. Blackmon. It's making you a fortune."

"I already have a fortune. Sell it and then buy up the competitor." He glanced at his notes. "Dream Images."

The broker grumbled, but Cain wasn't budging. He wasn't intent on ruining Kreeg, but he wasn't going to back a company whose CEO stalked and attacked women.

He cut the call and dialed a private investigator. Now that he had Phoebe's consent, he took control.

* * *

Phoebe knocked on the door, then peered around the edge. Cain was on the phone and looked more than a little irritated with the caller.

"If he's done this once, there is reason to believe he's done it before." He listened to the caller for a moment. "I'm betting there are more women out there, so find them. Fine, good." He hung up and looked at her. His expression softened.

"Thank you," she said.

"I haven't done anything yet."

"Yes, you have. You've given Kreeg a reason to be nervous. I take it this is all anonymous?"

"For anyone but my attorneys, yes. It has to be, for your sake. My name has mud on it, too."

Phoebe disagreed, but she wasn't going to try to persuade him otherwise. His name had fear on it. She wasn't surprised; he could be rather intimidating when he wanted to and on the phone with whoever that was, she could see he wasn't taking "I'll try my best," for an answer.

Phoebe admired someone so determined. But it made her wonder again, why, with all he had, he wouldn't face the world beyond Nine Oaks' walls. She was confident he'd trust her enough to tell her someday and she didn't want to press it. She'd seen the side of Cain she remembered and wanted to keep that close for as long as she could.

The thought made her realize that despite his life-style and that annoying way he could shut off his emotions, she was starting to fall for him again.

"So what are you up to now that it's raining?" he said.

A summer storm raged outside but they could barely hear it.

She shrugged, adjusting her V-neck top. She felt sluggish since she'd showered and slipped into soft jersey slacks and a top. "A feeble attempt at reading." She moved to leave. "I'll let you get back to work."

"Wait." Cain went to the antique sideboard and poured brandy into a snifter, then set it on the warmer.

Her brows knit as he waited for it to reach the per-fect temperature. "Don't leave."

Phoebe's heart leaped. He was usually telling her to get lost. "If that's for me, Cain, I don't need it."

"It's just a little brandy." He came to her. "Have a seat."

She dropped to the cushy sofa and he handed it to her. Then he knelt, his hands on either side of her hips on the cushion. "Your fear makes you so rest-less. Try sleeping. You look exhausted."

Three days here and she still hadn't slept, he

thought. What good was this fortress if she still didn't feel protected?

"I know," she said, "but I can't seem to rest for long."

"Try." He tipped the snifter to her lips and she sipped. "You're safe here. I won't let him touch you again. And in your dreams, he can't hurt you."

"But he does," she said weakly, her eyes tearing, her wounds showing so clearly, Cain's heart fractured a little.

"You give him power when you let him torment you," he said, brushing layers of hair off her forehead.

Phoebe fought the urge to turn her face into his palm. "I know." She sipped again, feeling the warm liquor soften her limbs. "I'd better leave you alone to work."

Her lids felt heavy.

She started to get up, but he kept her there, adjusting the pillows, then taking the finished brandy and easing her to lie down. "You'll wake up too much if you have to walk upstairs, so sleep right here."

"But you're working."

He pulled off her sandals, then grabbed an afghan from an old trunk to cover her. "It's all right," he said gently. "Close your eyes."

"Yes, m'lord." She obeyed.

He smiled with tender humor. "Imp."

"Ogre," she muttered, then sighed into the cushions.

Cain ached to touch her, to kiss her, but instead he stood, moving to sit behind his desk. He didn't make a sound, watching her. She looked so tiny on the long sofa. Despite her zest and energy, she was still hurting inside, still tormented. He could learn what Kreeg had done to her from the detectives and lawyers, but it was her private business. He'd wait in the hopes that she'd trust him and tell him herself.

He didn't even consider telling her about Lily. It was not the same. Phoebe was innocent. Cain was not.

He focused on work, routing all his calls to a machine. Occasionally he looked up, and was relieved that she was in a deep sleep.

After a while, he left her alone to rest. He met Benson in the hall, looking panicked.

"Sir, I can't find Miss Phoebe."

"She's sleeping." He inclined his head to the library.

Benson's brows shot up.

Cain ignored his shock. He was well aware that it was not his normal behavior to have anyone that close. "See that no one disturbs her till she wants to be."

Benson nodded, his stoic expression melting into a smile as he walked off.

* * *

It was near midnight when Cain scooped Phoebe up off the sofa and carried her upstairs. Her compact body felt fragile in his arms and the fact that she didn't stir much told him she was finally sleeping peacefully. He entered her suite where the bed was already turned down and laid her in the center, then drew the coverlet over her.

For her peace of mind, he locked the balcony doors, and windows, and he was tempted to post one of dogs at the foot of the bed, but didn't. He started to leave, then turned back, suddenly beside the bed, gazing down at her.

She stirs up a lot of trouble for someone so small, he thought. Then admitted he liked it. A lot more than he should. She brought life to this old house, and he'd missed that.

Without will he bent, and kissed her soft mouth. That she responded in her sleep stirred something deep in his heart.

That she whispered his name—touched his soul.

Seven

Cain asked himself what he was doing when he left the library for the third time in a day.

But he knew.

A dozen reasons to stay locked in his cave, as Phoebe called it, trotted through his mind. He'd tried to ignore the noise that broke his concentration, yet knowing she was near, bringing laughter to the dark lonely house, pushed him beyond the warnings.

A part of him hoped he didn't find her.

But he did, chatting in the solarium with Willis. The young man was laying out a lunch for her as

Phoebe sat on the garden sofa, her feet propped on the coffee table, a book on her lap. Her voice was animated as she talked to the young man, but Cain couldn't hear her clearly. Leaning his shoulder against the wide French doors, he simply watched her interact. It was truly pitiful that he was so fascinated by her expressive face.

Willis stepped back, talking softly as she teased him that Jean Claude obviously thought she was too thin if he expected her to eat all that food. Willis laughed, she smiled, and the entire room lit a little brighter.

Willis was enamored with her, and while jealousy pricked Cain, he also admired how Phoebe could put anyone at ease.

Then her gaze strayed past the young man and her smile widened. "I know your mama taught you that eavesdropping was impolite."

"Yes ma'am, she did."

Willis turned sharply, his posture stiffening, his gaze nervously shooting between Phoebe and his employer. Cain frowned, realizing again that the people who worked for him feared him. It made him more aware that, in the last years, he'd become a demanding taskmaster with little patience for anyone. These people didn't deserve it. Especially when his wrath was directed at himself.

He looked at the servant. "Relax, Willis," Cain said softly. "Why don't you take a break for a while." He stepped into the large room.

Willis's eyes rounded. "Sir?"

"Take off for the day. I'm sure we can fend for ourselves." He glanced at Phoebe and her smile was so dazzling, Cain swore nothing else was more beautiful.

"I beg your pardon, sir, and I don't mean to sound ungrateful, but Benson sets my duties and he might not like that."

Cain walked to the intercom and depressed the button, calling for Benson.

"Yes, sir."

"Give Willis the day off." The lad smiled. "In fact, give the entire staff the day off. With pay."

"I beg your pardon, sir?"

"Is there anything that can't be taken care of tomorrow?"

"Dinner, sir."

He glanced at Phoebe and winked. "We can manage. Anything else?"

"No sir, but…"

"Good lord, do I have to shove you people out the door?"

Willis snickered under his breath.

"Apparently, sir." Benson's voice came through

the speaker, clear with a touch of humor. "Very well, sir. Have a pleasant afternoon."

Cain bid him the same and clicked off the intercom. Willis nodded and left in a hurry, already pulling at his tie. Cain turned his gaze on Phoebe. She swung her legs off the coffee table and just stared at him.

"Bravo," she said softly. "I'm impressed."

That he hadn't paid attention to his staff's fear, or the busywork they did to keep themselves occupied, embarrassed Cain. "They hover," he said, as if that was the reason he wanted them gone.

"Come sit." She patted the space beside her. "Share this with me." She pointed to the tray of food. He moved toward her almost gracefully and settled beside her.

"No pressing work?"

"No, it's all done." It was a white lie, he always had work to do, but nothing that couldn't wait. "I'm a genius, didn't you know that?" he teased.

His playfulness wasn't as much of a shock as it was a few days ago. But Phoebe loved seeing it just the same. "I knew that years ago."

She split her sandwich and handed him half, then curled her legs on the sofa and took a bite. Cain set the plate between them, snatching at her chips, tasting the crab salad.

"So why'd you leave the cave?"

Only his eyes shifted to lock with hers. "I think you know why."

"Nope, I don't. If you mean to say you did it for me, I don't believe you."

"Why?"

"Because it was like pulling teeth to get you on the picnic."

Cain shrugged, unable to answer with anything that wouldn't open a door too wide. He thought about what he wanted, what he was keeping at bay. He wanted Phoebe and he needed his past to stay out of it.

If she knew, she'd leave instantly and he couldn't bear that.

"You're in here a lot."

She looked toward the ceiling, the tempered glass showing the afternoon sky. A paddle fan pushed the cooled air around the large room, swaying the flowers, surrounding them with fragrance. Beyond the glass, rain fell.

"It's like being outside without all the ick."

He arched a brow. "Gnats, the oppressive heat?"

"Nosy reporters sitting at the fence with long-range cameras."

Cain scowled and started to get up to see to the matter when she grabbed his hand.

"Let it go. It won't do any good. They'll just find another way."

Cain begged to differ, yet he eased back into the seat, finishing off the sandwich and looking for more.

She offered him hers. He shook his head.

"You want it," she teased, "you know you do." She held it closer.

"There are other things I want more."

"Oh?" she said, suddenly breathless and reading the velvety look in his eyes.

"Yeah, your chips." As he said that, he munched into one.

She grinned, then ate the sandwich in record time.

He blinked. "Glad I didn't really want more."

"Hey, you had your chance."

"You have mayonnaise on your mouth."

She licked her lip and the slow slide of her tongue over her lips felt like a charge to Cain. The woman was too deliciously sexy and when she reached for a napkin, Cain leaned forward, swift and stark like a hunter seeking its prey.

"I'll take care of that," he murmured, then kissed her.

Phoebe melted, instantly, completely. His tongue snaked over her lips, outlining them so provocatively she felt at once unhinged and desperate for more. He tasted her, and she savored each nuance of the kiss—the way his lips worked over her, his rushed breathing—and when he applied pressure she leaned back, pulling him on the sofa with her.

He deepened his kiss, taking it from the soft, erotic exploration to total possession. His mouth moved heavily, passion rising swiftly through her until she couldn't contain it.

His hand slid under her, lifting her hips to his, his erection pressing deeply and eliciting a moan for more. Yes, she thought, more. She wanted him, and her response left no question between them. She'd wanted this for years, aching in her soul to know if passion was all they had, and Phoebe knew, even as her heart tumbled, even as his hands swept her body to cup her breast, this was the passion of a lifetime.

She clawed at his shoulders, urging him yet feeling his resistance, and when he broke the kiss, staring down at her, Phoebe wondered what was going on in his mind.

Then she knew.

"I want to touch you. No, I need to," he said, nipping at her mouth, her throat and lower. "You excite me more than anything."

"That's a good thing then," she said, smiling and tipping her head back as he nibbled his way lower.

"I didn't think anything would stir you from that place you keep yourself in."

Instantly she regretted the comment when his gaze flashed up and she saw it again, that self-recrimination. A dark burden, like a demon looming ready to pounce, and she leaned up and kissed him, forcing it from his mind, drawing him back to the moment, the passion bubbling between them.

Cain went willingly, eager for anything to keep guilt at bay and indulge in her. He never broke the kiss, making her breathless, stealing her will as she stole his.

His hand crept under her shirt, a finger hooking the edge of her bra and pulling.

Phoebe was more than eager, and pulled her shirt up, letting him unhook her. His hand played over her breast, pushing the bra aside and he savored the feel of her smooth skin beneath his palms.

When his lips closed over her nipple, she made a little sound and arched into him. He shifted, pulling her onto his lap, then spreading her thighs so she straddled him. She smiled at him and he stripped off her shirt, the bra. His mouth was on her, laving her flesh. He suckled and massaged and she arched back, gripping his shoulder and Cain watched her passion rise, stroked her smooth skin, feeling the weight of her breast so warm in his hands. His fingers trailed lower and he dipped below the waistband of her thin jersey slacks. Her muscles contracted and she straightened, meeting his gaze.

"Can I touch you?"

Phoebe was incredibly moved by that, the trickle of fear in his voice, that she might turn him away. "I wish you would."

His lips quirked, half arrogant half delighted and he shifted his hand, his fingertip stroking her soft center through her panties. Her breath rushed in sharply and she whispered, "More," then kissed him.

Cain devoured her sweet mouth as he dipped his hand under the band of her panties and touched her heat. His fingertips slid wetly over her delicate flesh and she shivered in his arms, made a tight little sound and flexed her hips.

Then he plunged a finger inside her. She inhaled and cupped his face, staring into his eyes as he explored and teased. "Cain, oh Cain."

"You have to let me see it. It's been haunting me for years, Phoebe." He didn't give her a choice and withdrew and plunged, feeling vulnerable himself as he touched her, scented her like a stag on the prowl. Her passion was overpowering, her slick body throbbing against his touch and when he circled the delicate pearl of her sex, she thrust hard against him.

He gave her what she wanted, what he needed to

see, to experience. It was as if this were a little flash
of light in a dark tunnel. His own body was hard and
ready; it would be so easy to open his trousers and
drive into her. He throbbed to do it. To be primal and
raw with her. To feel her lush body grasp him, take
him. He wanted her so much that when he felt her
tensing, he nearly climaxed.

He plunged and flicked, and stroked, aware of her
every quiver, her staggered breath. Wet heat coated
him. It was as if he'd known the workings of her body
for years and how to pull the sensations from her. She
was wild in his arms, flexing in erotic rhythm to his
touch.

And then she found it, capturing his soul as she
contracted and shivered in his arms. Her scattered
breaths sounded in his ear, and he knew he'd never
forget it, never banish this from his mind for it felt
as if he were holding daylight. She tensed hard, then
collapsed against him, and Cain could only gather
her tightly and feel the shudders of her desire fold
around his heart and take him prisoner.

Phoebe tried to catch her breath, tried to find logic
and reason why he wanted to do that to her so badly,
then just gave up and accepted it.

After a long moment, she lifted her head and met
his gaze.

He arched a brow, a bit of arrogant pleasure in his soft smile.

"Is that why you sent everyone away?"

His smile dropped a little. "No." He removed his hand, smoothing her spine. "Though the thought had crossed my mind."

She smiled widely and bent to kiss him. As if they'd never touched, the fire sparked. Like wind on flames, it grew and Phoebe slipped her hand between them molding his erection pushing against his tailored slacks.

Cain groaned and held her back. "Phoebe, don't."

"Why?"

"I'm about to explode and as much as I want to have you, we cannot go further."

She blinked. "Excuse me?"

He didn't like the anger in her eyes, didn't want to be the cause of it.

"Was that just satisfying your curiosity? Don't answer, forget I said that." She shifted off his lap, snatched up her clothes and dressed.

"You're angry with me."

"No, I'm hurt."

"Didn't you like it? I did."

She cast a glance over her shoulder. "Didn't I look like I enjoyed that? I am, however, feeling like a plaything right now."

She stood and started to leave. Cain shot off the sofa and grabbed her hand, ignoring the intense pain and hardness in his body and turning her toward him.

"You would never be a plaything to me, Phoebe. You have to know that. Tell me you know."

Phoebe sighed, not wanting to end this with a fight, not wanting to really dig deep into his mind when she didn't want anyone digging into hers. Then she noticed the torn look in his dark eyes, in his expression. Something was eating him. It made him look raw and desolate as he waited for her answer.

"Maybe without meaning to."

"There are no maybes about it."

"But then where will this go? Moments for a couple of weeks? Is that it?"

His gaze thinned and she knew she'd just touched a nerve.

"I understand now. You won't *allow* yourself to have more, with me, or anyone and I'm not just talking sex."

His expression went shuttered.

That he did it so often she could recognize it angered her. "Don't do that! Don't leave me out in the cold. Can't we just take this new stage one day at a time?"

Cain went still, a battle waging inside him—push the door a little wider open or pull it closed. Yet he knew one thing—with Phoebe, he had little choice. She was an energy he couldn't ignore.

He forced a smile, pulling her close, and smoothing her wild hair out of her eyes.

"One day at a time then." He didn't say it would go no further than her stay here at Nine Oaks until the trial. That, he knew, was enough heartache for the both of them.

Oblivious to his thoughts, Phoebe smiled widely and pecked a kiss to his mouth. "I won't even expect a miracle, I swear."

That, Cain thought, was what he needed—and did not deserve.

Something had changed between them. Neither one spoke of it, but Phoebe could feel it. His guard was down a little further. A line blurred when he cooked for her. It faded when he smiled and laughed and teased like the man she remembered.

"You didn't want to take over for your father?"

"Not really. It was always expected of me, but I would've liked to have made another choice."

"Such as?

He shrugged, sitting in the lounge chair on the balcony, watching the mist of the evening roll over the river. Cain turned his gaze from it, the scenery too much like the night Lily died.

"I'm not sure."

"Well, if you don't have a choice waiting, and I'm not saying you have to, then keep running the family companies. You're great at what you do, Cain."

"And you know this how?"

"I bought stock in your company."

He frowned. "I'll have to check the stockholders' list."

"I'm small potatoes." She sipped a mimosa and stretched on the lounge. The sounds of the night approached—music for them—and Phoebe looked over at him and found him staring.

He was trying not to be obvious but she could tell. He seemed to be comparing her to something when he looked at her. Then she remembered what he'd said that night in the kitchen. Not to think he was so noble that he was mourning his dead wife, that she'd be disappointed.

"Did you love Lily?"

His gaze snapped to hers. He hesitated before answering. "No. Barely."

She sat up a little straighter. "Then why did you marry her?"

"She was pregnant with my child."

"Oh."

"She miscarried a couple of weeks after we married."

"I'm so sorry. Did that happen when she died?"

"No. Do we have to discuss her?" He said *her* as if it tasted foul.

"I'm trying to understand you better. You're not making it easy, you know." He scowled and she took another avenue. "I, on the other hand, am an open book."

He chuckled, but it held little humor. "You have your secrets, too, pixie."

She flashed him a smile and lay back, drawing her leg up and resting her glass there. "What do you want to know?"

"What gives you nightmares?"

He saw her fingers grip the glass a little tighter and she took a huge sip. "I've been loud again?"

"I'm afraid so." He'd come into her room the night before when he'd heard her cry out with such fear it left a mark in his heart. Despite her brave front, the dreams tormented her nearly every night.

She groaned, and put the glass down, then rubbed her face. Cain left his chair and went to her, nudging her legs aside and sat on the end of the lounge.

She wouldn't look at him, and he touched beneath her chin and forced her to meet his gaze. "It's not my business, so don't think you must tell me a thing." But Cain could see the memories clouding her eyes and prepared himself.

She took a deep breath, then let it out and when she spoke, her voice was dry and monotone, as if she had told this story many times before. He suspected she had. "Randall and I dated a few times and he was nice enough, spending way too much money on the dates, but there was something about him that gave me the creeps. I couldn't point a finger at it, but it was there. So I broke it off and everything changed."

"He stalked you."

"No, not at first. He'd show up at my place and want to come in. Then he'd appear at the strangest places, and since we knew some of the same people, I couldn't attribute it to stalking." She sat up, drawing her legs cross-legged. "But he'd butt into conversations, touch me. You know, behaving like the boyfriend, and of course, no one would say anything to him because he was popular, and admired and rich." She turned her gaze to the water. "I went to his place to tell him to back off and he had pictures of me all over the place."

"Good God."

"Yeah. Beautifully framed, I might add. That's when I knew for sure he was dangerous."

She fidgeted and Cain grasped her hand. She gripped back and met his gaze. Tears wet her eyes but never fell.

"I called the police but since he hadn't hurt me,

they couldn't do much." She swallowed, the memories crowding in on her and she moistened her lips. "He grew bolder, more arrogant, as if nothing could touch him."

"How so?"

"He left a rose on my car seat, yet my car had been locked. The alarm didn't go off, either. The police suspected he took my keys and made copies."

She pulled free and ran her fingers through her hair. Cain could feel the tension rising in her and wanted to stop her, but she kept going.

"Then I heard sounds. At night. I would get up to investigate and find a window open when I knew I'd locked it. It was stuff like that for a while, then one night, he was in my bedroom."

Cain stiffened. "Excuse me?"

His tone went suddenly dangerous, cutting, and she met his gaze. "I woke in the middle of the night and he was standing over my bed."

"My God, Phoebe, what did you do?"

"I screamed, and he bailed out the window. The police found footprints outside. He'd been there for a while, watching me." The fear that he'd get out and start again had kept her awake nights.

"Why didn't they arrest him?"

"I didn't get a clear look at his face in the dark so I couldn't say it was him for sure."

She shivered, despite the warm evening and Cain shifted closer and rubbed her arms and shoulders. "But you knew it was."

She went into his arms without missing a beat.

"I changed the locks, and my phone number, and signed a restraining order, but when I stepped out of the shower, he was there. He said he belonged there. That I belonged to him."

"Did he touch you?"

Suddenly Phoebe had a death grip on his arm, and Cain pulled her across his lap, holding her tightly. "Phoebe?"

"Yes, yes! All over." Phoebe closed her eyes, trying to banish the memory of that man's hands on her skin, the ugly way he groped her. "He would have done…more if I hadn't fought him. He ran from the house and I called the police, but Randall had worked up a nice alibi and it couldn't be disputed right away." She was hoping her lawyer could do that at the trial. "I looked like a neurotic paranoid fool after that. I felt like I was the criminal. They had a cruiser drive by at night, but I was so scared I couldn't sleep at all." Her voice wavered and Cain felt immersed in her emotions. "Thank God one of the detectives believed me, and on his own time he sat outside my place."

"When did they catch him?"

She stared at her fingers, one of his making slow circles on the back of her hand. It was so incredibly soothing, she thought, and the words came easily.

"When he held a knife to my throat." Cain tensed against her and she could feel his anger rising. She met his gaze. "He was outside in the dark when I went to put out the trash one night. He said if he couldn't have me, no one would." She let out a slow trembling breath. "Then he forced me back inside. The police were there, watching, and I didn't think they'd get inside in time. They did, but not before he cut me." She flicked at the curls on her neck to show him the scar.

Good God, it was at her jugular.

Cain bent and kissed it, then sheltered her in his arms. Phoebe inhaled his scent, curled into him and her fear began to slide away.

"He's going to jail," Cain murmured, wanting Kreeg to pay dearly for this.

"Don't talk about that. I don't want to, not anymore. Kiss me, Cain, I need you."

He did.

Deeply, hotly. And she curled into his body, loving when his hands rode up her thighs, her hips, then under her shirt. He cupped her breasts, his fingertips smoothing the delicate lace of her bra and his kiss grew stronger. The skies unleashed, water drenching them in seconds, yet his hand slipped between her thighs. She pressed him to her warm center and he rubbed, aching to have her bare beneath his touch again, to hear her cries when she climaxed for him.

"Oh, Cain."

"I want you." Madly, desperately, he thought.

"Me, too. I have for nine years."

He hesitated. "I'm not the same man."

"That's a good thing," she whispered, smiling, and wanted to be lying with him not across his lap.

Cain didn't think so, and with her cradled in his arms, he stood and walked with her through the silent house.

"Are we going where I think we are?" she said, and he liked the lightness in her tone, but couldn't allow himself to fall for it.

"No. You're going to bed." She made a face, looping her arms around his neck.

He entered her suite and laid her on the center of the bed, covering her.

"Alone?"

Good grief, the woman could tempt a saint and Cain wondered when his resolve would shatter. "Sleep, Phoebe, you've had enough for one night."

"You're babying me."

"I want to, let me. Sleep, no one will hurt you. I'll be right here." He pulled a chair close and sat.

"You could be right here," she said, yawning hugely and plucking at the bedsheets.

He gnashed his teeth, thinking he was damn noble, and wished she'd just conk out before he got stupid.

Like a charm, the earlier cocktail sent her into sleep quickly, and Cain stretched his long frame out in the chair that was too delicate for his size.

As if waiting till she was most vulnerable, Kreeg invaded her dreams. She twisted, again trying to crawl away. Then she kicked out violently, flinched and gasped, and Cain could only imagine the details of her trauma as he quickly came to her, braving her flailing fists to gather her in his arms. She made a pitiful, angry sound and he whispered her name and how he'd never let anyone hurt her again. She didn't wake, yet a tear slid down her cheek. He drew her into the curve of his body, his arms wrapped tightly as he lay down on the bed. After a moment she settled, calling his name in a whimper that cut through to his bones.

Cain squeezed his eyes shut, hurting for her, and offered her the only thing he could: soft whispers and his strength. When he wanted to give her the world.

Eight

Phoebe was descending the stairs, dressed in Suzannah's old riding habit when she saw Cain.

She smiled, her heart doing a little dance as she neared. Nobody made her feel the way he did. His dark looks and angled features were to die for, but it was his soulful eyes that got to her. They seemed to dig into her heart and make a home there, and beg her to set him free from this self-imposed prison.

Last night, he'd held her through her dreams, keeping her safe from them, and she'd never felt so protected and cherished. He'd become her port in her private storm. She wished she could be that for him.

"Out again?" he said, leaning on the banister and looking more relaxed than ever.

"I have at least five acres I haven't seen yet."

"It's just fields."

"I know, but it's neat to see them filled with crops." He made a sour face, and she gave him a playful shove. "You've been around it all your life, you take it for granted. But the food and textiles have grown here on the same land for hundreds of years. Sort of unusual nowadays."

He stared thoughtfully. "The strangest things amuse you."

"I know. I'm a cheap date." She stopped on the last step at his eye level and met his gaze. Her entire body ached for him, her mouth tingling to be kissed. "Join me?" She'd asked before, but he never had.

Cain thought for a second, the temptation of being alone with her far outweighing the reasons he shouldn't. "In about a half hour?" He flicked at the sheaf of papers he held.

Her expression lit with excitement, making her eyes bright. "Really? I'll ask Mr. Dobbs to saddle Pegasus. Shall I wait or meet you?"

"By the stream. It's going to rain again, though, so we won't have a long ride."

"I'll take what I can get." She leaned and kissed him softly.

Cain's hand immediately gripped her waist and pulled her off the last step and into his arms. The papers fell to the floor as Phoebe sank into him. His mouth moved heavily over hers, his hands expressing his banked passion as they slid up her rib cage, her back and pressed her ever harder.

Phoebe wanted to drag him into the nearest room and explore this with him.

Then someone cleared his throat.

Cain drew back slowly, his breathing labored, and he loved that she didn't open her eyes right away, as if savoring the sensations that exploded between them.

Then they both looked toward the sound.

Benson stood near the door, actually smiling, a riding helmet in his hand.

Phoebe didn't say a word except to brush her lipstick off his lips, then went to Benson, taking the helmet.

"I'll be waiting," she said with a glance back, her eyes begging him not to disappoint her.

Cain wouldn't.

Or at least he didn't mean to, but a half hour later, he walked to the stable in time to see her riderless horse trot toward him.

He groaned. She was going to be mad, he thought, grabbing the mount's reins. Dobbs rushed out to take the animal, and then looked around.

"Where's Miss Phoebe, sir?"

Cain's gaze shot to the saddled horse, the stables, then to Dobbs. "She's not here already?" Cain asked carefully, his heartbeat skipping when he realized the mount was winded.

"You saw, sir. The horse came back without her."

"Oh, God." Cain ran into the stable and was astride his stallion and leaping out the exit before Dobbs could say more. At breakneck speed, he headed to the stream, panic racing harder with the pounding of the horse's hooves. His imagination tortured him with a short burst of dangerous pictures as he rounded a curve, branches swiping at his clothes.

Overhead the black clouds formed and collided, threatening to unleash their wrath before he found her.

Then he did, on her back under a tree, and his heart tumbled to his stomach as he yanked back on the reins. The horse reared, pawed the air, then dropped its hooves to the ground with a hard thump as Cain threw himself off and raced to her.

"Phoebe!" He grabbed her up in his arms. "Are you all right? Are you hurt?"

"No. I'm fine. My dignity's bruised, though."

Cain let out a long breath, clutching her tightly, realizing exactly how terrified he was, how much she meant to him. Then he showed her, cupping her face and kissing her wildly.

She responded instantly, and the power of his kiss drove her head back, her body arching into his. Heat bubbled and flowed between them, the wind doing nothing to cool the passion that boiled over and took them with it. Cain tasted her like a madman, a starved man, and he knew he was. She was an addiction, a deep need in his heart that cried out to be satisfied. Having more of her would never be enough, yet his mind warned him that the tempest would erupt and there would be no stopping it.

"You've scared the life out of me three times," he said fiercely against her mouth, then kissed her again.

The dogs, at the river, and now this, she thought. "Yeah, I know."

He cupped her jaw and met her gaze. *"Stop it."*

Phoebe saw real fear for her in his eyes. "I'm sorry. It wasn't intentional."

"I know. I know... What happened?"

"A branch knocked me back and I lost my seat."

He peppered her face with kisses, wanting to take her to the ground and have her now. "Thank God, you weren't thrown."

"Tell that to my butt."

He smiled against her mouth. "Want me to rub it?"

"Oh yes, please." His gaze slid to hers and her expression went sly and sexy. "Never offer if you aren't ready to do it."

He hands slid from her waist, cupped her behind, and massaged gently.

"Oh man," she said, and he groaned with her. She wiggled against him, wanting to stay right there.

"This opens a door, Phoeb."

She framed his face in her tiny hands. "Been open for a long time, Cain." Her tongue snaked out to lick his lips. "Stop knocking and walk through." The challenge turned her green eyes smoky.

"Good God, I didn't need to hear that," he said, but the temptation of Phoebe DeLongpree was more than any man should have to suffer. He ducked his head, and laid his mouth luxuriously over hers again. Overhead, the sky darkened, and storm clouds rumbled inland from the river as he tasted her.

Rain fell. Lightning cracked and she flinched. Cain dragged himself from her arms and went to the horse, climbing up, then tipped his booted foot out. She placed hers on his instep and he leaned, slipped his arm around her waist, and hoisted her up to deposit her on his lap, side saddle.

"So gallant," she said, and shivered dramatically.

"We're going to get drenched again," he murmured against her lips, then drank her in again.

She nipped at his lower lip, her desire for him pounding with the thunder. "It's just water."

Things were so simple for her, he thought as he nudged the horse toward home.

But the motion of the horse ground her behind into his groin. Cain shifted her, mumbling under his breath.

"I'm too heavy."

"No, you're making me...insane."

"Yeah, I can feel it," she teased, and his eyes darkened, the strain showing in his features. "You'll be ready for the loony bin soon."

Rain splashed over them, water dripping down his handsome face. His gaze was coal-black and intense, and Phoebe felt a tidal wave of emotions at the powerful stare. He seemed on the brink of something, his body tense, edgy.

"Save me then," he said. More than just teasing, more than a consent between them, his words held a desperate plea for her. He'd denied himself the pleasures of people, of simple delights, and while Phoebe wanted to solve the reasons, she simply kissed him.

And he possessed her. The passion they'd shared before rose fast and furiously to a new height, a new place and Phoebe felt swallowed whole and consumed down to her heels.

He stretched her across his lap, his hand hurriedly

mapping her curves, dipping between her thighs to rub and tease. Rain melted over them, into their kiss and Phoebe drove her fingers into his hair and held him, telling him she wanted more, wanted anything he did. And in the kiss, she let all her doubts fall away and soak into the ground with the falling rain.

She hungered for him, and while she knew in her heart her own feelings, she didn't dare bring them out. He would hurt her again and she asked herself, "Will you risk hurt for him?" And her heart shouted, "Yes."

Cain let go of the reins to hold her, his hands skimming her impatiently from breast to thigh and back again. Phoebe arched in his embrace, the horse jolted and Cain gripped her, laughing and curling her around him.

"Good God, we'll end up in the mud."

"Hmm…kinky."

He chuckled darkly and laid his mouth over hers again, his tongue slipping between her lips and teasing her with the motion. Near the stable, the horse quickened its pace and Cain tore his mouth from hers and drew on the reins.

In the pouring rain, he met her gaze, and she could see the question in his eyes. Did she want to take this further?

She touched his jaw and in a single kiss answered, begged to be fulfilled. Right now.

He eased her down, then hopped off as Dobbs rushed out.

"Oh, thank the lord you're all right, Miss Phoebe."

She glanced at the man, smiled. "I am, Mr. Dobbs, thank you."

Quickly, Cain positioned her in front of him. "Please don't move."

She twisted a look at Cain, amused, and feeling the evidence of their playing pressing warmly to her behind. "Now would I do that to my rescuer?"

"You'd do anything to tease me."

Oblivious, Dobbs took the reins and led the horse away, saying, "Gonna be a big storm. Best get out of it and them wet clothes before y'all get sick."

Cain winked at her. "Yes, we best."

She grinned. "Race yah," she said and she shot toward the house.

Cain blinked, staring after her, then chased her down. He caught her in the mudroom, snagging her around the waist, and went crazy kissing her.

"Here? Oh fun," she said, working off her muddy boots.

"Hell no, but I have to touch you. Everywhere."

Excitement coursed through her as Cain toed off his boots, then grasped her hand, pulling her into the house. He paused in the back hall, looking around.

"You're sparing my reputation, how sweet."

He glanced. "I should send them all home."

"Do." She slid her hand provocatively over his flat stomach, her fingertips grazing his erection. "I plan to be vocal."

"Oh God," Cain groaned and swept her up in his arms, bolting toward the staircase and taking the steps two at a time.

Phoebe laughed at his enthusiasm and he silenced her with a kiss at the top of the stairs, then let her legs go. She stood on her toes, her body pressed against his, his back to the wall. His hands were busy redis-covering her contours, enfolding her breasts to thumb her nipples in deep circles through her wet shirt. She whimpered and leaned into his touch, yanking his shirt from his trousers, and driving her hands up his bare chest. He made a growling sound of such dark hunger, Phoebe felt empowered.

Then the sound of voices floated up from down-stairs.

"Oh no, spies," he whispered, then wiggled his brows.

Phoebe was captivated by the freedom in his smile, and when he pulled her toward the west wing and the wide double doors of the master suite, she didn't hesitate. The antiques, and the opulent decor blurred around her. All she saw was Cain. How, in his own way, he cared deeply for her. He'd limited himself for five years, but now, he wasn't. Then outside the doors, he stopped and looked at her intently.

"Are you sure? Nothing will be the same."

She gazed up at him, seeing how greedy he was for her and knew it mirrored her own passion. If nothing came of this beyond one night, she told herself, it was a precious moment in time she would cherish and accept.

"I'm sure, Cain. Are you?"

"I don't think there is a question in my mind that I couldn't reason away, but God help me, I want you so badly." At the last word, his mouth came down on hers and he backed up and nudged the door open, then maneuvered her inside.

He kicked the door closed behind them, drawing back to look her in the eye. Something had changed. Phoebe felt him quake, the restrained power in his tall body, and it thrilled her. She touched the side of his face, her feelings and her desire for him overwhelming her. He was so handsome, and so different right now. His damp hair was wildly mussed, far from the well-manicured way he'd looked when she'd first seen him. His clothing was wet and muddy, and he appeared more rugged than elegant, more real than the fearsome beast she'd met two weeks ago.

"I like you like this," she said, gripping his belt and tugging him near. "Messy, relaxed."

"I'm far from relaxed."

"Oh?" She opened the buckle.

"I feel like I'm about to crack in half." He smoothed his hands over her hair and cradled her face. "I'm almost afraid to let go."

Something tightened around her heart, clamping down hard and squeezing her breathless.

"I don't want to hurt you."

But you will, she thought. *You won't leave Nine Oaks and that hurts me. Hurts us.*

Yet she said nothing, leaning into his body, and he snatched her up, kissing her madly, the force of it bending her back over his arm.

"You taste so good," he murmured. "I can't wait. I can't."

His gaze traveled over her as she stood stretched out to him, nearly limp under his touch, and his hand moved up to her waist, savoring the feel of her cool damp skin before he slipped under her shirt and filled his palm with her breast. She made a sweet sound and he pushed the wet shirt and bra upward, baring her to the heat of his mouth. Warm lips met her cool flesh and she shrieked at the contact, then moaned as he laved, his lips tugging at her nipple, sending tight clawing desire spiraling outward.

He kept tasting and the feelings magnified and blossomed.

She let him have what he wanted, loving the fierceness of his touch, the gentleness of his embrace. She crossed her arms, pulling her shirt off and dropping it to the floor. The bra followed. She straightened and worked her slacks off.

Cain was treated to the erotic sight of peeling fabric and flawless flesh. It left him incapable of moving, his gaze ripping over her. She wore only a black thong. She moved closer, unfastening his shirt buttons, but Cain couldn't be bothered and tore off his shirt, popping buttons in his eagerness to feel her skin next to his.

Phoebe was almost stunned by the sight of his body. The muscles molded his frame like sculptured ropes of power, flexing as he tossed aside the shirt.

"What?" he said when she stared.

"You don't sit behind a desk all the time."

"I have a lot of time on my hands.".

Now he was hers. He was her prisoner, and she explored him, her hands gliding delicately over his skin. The simple act tightened his grip on her waist. Then she slicked her tongue across his nipple and he trembled for her.

She pulled his belt free, swinging it once before she dropped it, then sent his zipper down. His hands curled into fists, knuckles popping, and she could taste the tension in him, see it in the flex of his jaw. He was hard perfection and this would be fast and heated, she knew. There was nothing stopping their first taste of each other and she planned on it going on for a while.

Forever, if she had a choice. The thought made her still for a second.

"Phoebe."

"There are no rules, Cain. Not with us."

Then her hand dipped inside his trousers, and she enfolded him. He slammed his eyes shut, throwing his head back with a deep growl of male pleasure. His throat worked, his arousal flexed in her hand.

She stroked him, pushing his trousers down and he looked at her, pulling her hand free.

"I won't make it," he said honestly and was surprised he had any control left.

He kissed her, his hands sweeping her ripe body, teasing her with a dip and stroke, then slipping inside her panties and toying with her center. Her breathing increased, and Cain wanted more of her, needed her so desperately and for a moment, he wondered how he'd survived all these years without her.

Then he gripped the delicate thong, and tugged. It popped and he tossed it aside.

"Oh, you enjoyed that."

"Every man's fantasy? You betcha."

He moved forward till her back was braced on the bedpost, the giant Rice bed looming beyond, tempting them with wild play. But Cain wanted to have his fantasy with Phoebe, to play out the dreams that had been torturing him since she walked through the door again. His hands on her waist slid upward, coasting under her arms and pushing them high. Then he wrapped her hands around the carved post. "Hold on."

"I'll need to?"

"Yeah." His look was savagely erotic with promise. "Don't let go."

She smiled, and he bent and took her nipple deep into the hot suck of his mouth. She inhaled and moaned, arching and with his knee, he spread her thighs, his fingers sliding warmly and smoothly, teasing her with light pressure. She was vocal, telling him how good that felt, wanting more, deeper, longer strokes, and her hips thrust into his touch. But he wouldn't give her what she wanted, not enough to satisfy her, and she was panting, begging him.

It was exactly what he wanted. She was a strong woman, candid and outspoken, and Cain had little power. Here he did.

He discovered her, what made her squirm, what brought her closer to the edge of a climax. His mouth found the sweet under-curve of her breast, the ticklish spot on her ribs, and he heard her gasp when he dragged his tongue down the line of muscle to her navel.

He swirled and licked, and her legs softened. She gripped the post. "Cain. Oh Cain."

He ran his hand over her behind, pausing to dip into her and stroke her liquid center, then he curled his long fingers around her knee, and lifted it to his shoulder.

"Oh my sweet heaven," she gasped.

He left nothing to chance, no inch of her delectable skin untouched. His broad hands splayed her hips, thumbs teasing her center. He looked up, met her stormy gaze, then peeled her open.

He tasted her.

She slammed her eyes shut, her breath tumbling as he pleasured her. Years alone had not dimmed his expertise, but made him precise and intense. In seconds, she was close, and he possessed the bead of her sex in every way. He brought her near and receded, chuckling when she demanded, when she told him this was divine and he'd get his.

"You first," he growled when she was shivering, till her breathing was fast and hot. Till her body glistened with sweat.

Then he plunged two fingers inside and pushed her over the edge of rapture.

She climaxed beautifully, a ribbon of femininity bending, her body flexing and pawing beneath his touch.

"Cain. Cain!"

He didn't answer, silent in his assault, loving how she spoke of her feelings, of what he did to her body, her heart. And the cries, oh yes, the cries were like music to his ears.

She'd yet to settle past the pulse of her climax, was still in the throes of it when Cain stood, sweeping an arm around her and pulling her with him onto the bed. He shucked his trousers, his erection fiercely hard, and she curled toward him, her hand sliding over his body, pulling him onto her.

"Cain. Now."

He produced a condom and she applied it deftly, quickly, watching his eyes flare, feeling him elongate for her. Her throat went tight again, and she kissed him.

"Now," she said. "Please."

"Yes, now." He plunged deeply, filling her in one smooth stroke.

She felt his trembling all the way to her spine.

He slammed his eyes shut, the pulse of her body trapping him more than he could bear.

When he opened his eyes she was staring at him, then pressed her forehead to his, rasping her thumb over his lips as she said, "I feel like I've waited an eternity for this."

Shock and pleasure riddled him. "Me, too."

The need to move took them, stole her breath as she rose and came back to him.

Gone was the tortured emotion he hid. With each plunge came a new man, the one she knew before life was cruel to his heart. He braced a hand on the head-board and held her gaze as he left her and pushed home. She wrapped her legs around his hips, and pulled him deeper, wanting him harder, faster, but he was intent on her pleasure, on satisfying her when she knew he was ready to explode.

The wet slide of him pulsed with savage desire. Their pace quickened. The bed shook, their climax rushing ahead of them.

Cain wanted to slow down but it was impossible. He thirsted, his need to claim her, if only this way, was rooted in his being. Not in sex.

His hips pistoned, her body a slick glove pulling pleasure from him. She splayed her hands on his chest, taunting him with words, with her hands.

She hid nothing from him, open and bare, and for a moment, they watched him disappear into her. He met her gaze, loving that she was not timid, that she was herself in all aspects. Her boldness was part of her, her need to find freedom in everything, and Cain clutched her close to his heart, hoping to know it, share it. Even when he knew he would not.

Their gazes locked, the searing heat destroying his reservations about himself, her, his life.

"This will never be enough," he said. "Never."

"I know. I know."

And he lowered onto her, cupping her buttocks and rolling to his back with her locked to him.

She rose up, smiling, knowing she had the power and he gave it to her.

On a mound of pillows, Cain enjoyed the splendor of her, leaning up to capture her nipple. Her hips shot forward, her body sliding slickly onto his. She gripped his shoulders, holding his gaze, her quick breaths, her tender pleas to join her were enough to destroy him. He was there, sheer will keeping the explosion back and he dribbled his hands down her body and touched the bead of her sex with infinite care. She slammed down onto him and found rapture.

The eruption tore through them with bone-racking power. The pound of bodies tore passion from its cage and Cain gripped her, grinding her to him and she answered the push, equal in her pleasure, her need, her demand.

He cried out her name.

She cupped his face, and thrust, experiencing his pleasure, watched it darken his eyes, turn them liquid wild, releasing all he kept banked from the world.

Feminine muscles tightened, and his shattering pulse made him buck. She held on, suspended and fused with him, and they clutched for long breathless moments, riding the wave of their pleasure.

Phoebe collapsed on him, breathing hard, and Cain held her, silent, his chest aching with emotions he didn't want to examine. He kissed her hair, her cheek, and when she lifted her head to look at him, there was a tear in her eye.

"Phoebe?"

"I knew it would be like this, you know."

He stared for a moment, thinking of lies he might tell, ways to keep his heart out of this, but right now, he couldn't. "Yeah, I think, so did I."

She laid her head down and sighed, and Cain felt at once free and chained tighter to his past.

Nine

Cain stood on the balcony outside the master suite, staring at the moon glistening on the river. The view was spectacular, despite the shifting storm clouds threatening to unleash again. Yet a gale raged inside him and he glanced back at the bed.

The air-conditioning stirred the drapes, revealing the tiny beauty sprawled in his bed. The last few hours bloomed in his mind with the power to leave him hungry for more of her.

What have I done?

Cain didn't regret the last hours; the passion between them was unlike anything he'd experienced before with any woman.

But then, he knew it would be.

It was the reason he'd avoided her since that first kiss under the stairs. She consumed him, and he felt almost obsessed with having her again. Always. He could spend a lifetime with her, and he'd never have enough of her sweet, vibrant energy.

But morning would bring reality, he thought, and when she stirred on the sheets, he was reluctant to speak to her.

To end it.

He forced himself to move toward her, tugging the sash of his robe. She rolled to her back, her bare body seductively draped in sheets.

"I'm hungry. Feed me."

He chuckled to himself and settled on the edge of the bed. She sat up and scooted close, her slender arms sliding around his neck. She kissed him, the heat gathering and stealing Cain's will. With a groan, he deepened the kiss and drew her across his lap, running his hand upward from her thigh till he cupped her bare breast. He rolled her nipple under his thumb, feeling it peak deliciously for him.

She arched into his touch, gasping for air. "I'm *really* hungry."

"So am I."

He pushed her to her back, his warm mouth laving over her breast, drawing on her nipple. She curled toward him, as if all her nerves were locked between his lips.

"Cain, Cain." Frantically, she searched the bedsheets for a condom packet.

His hand slipped between her thighs, fingers sliding and teasing. "You're so beautiful when you're like this." She was spread wide and uninhibited, letting him see every curve, feel every sensation he created in her.

"Now," was all she said, tearing at his sash. She enfolded him, sheathing him as he moved between her thighs.

"Phoebe." He hadn't meant for it to go this far.

He thrust, burying himself in her, and she arched passionately, then jerked back till he left her completely. He plunged again. And again.

And she coaxed him faster, her hands taunting his restraint, and braced above her, Cain withdrew and answered the rushing passion.

They were savage, flesh meeting flesh and melting into one stream of heat and desire. He was afraid he'd hurt her yet she answered him, wild and erotic. The clash pushed them across the bed till she was gripping the headboard and begging him to let go. He gripped her hips bringing her to him, a passionate command quickly taking them over the edge of passion and into a spine-tingling climax.

His gaze never left hers. Her eyes expressed her desire, and something more. Something he'd longed to see in a woman—in Phoebe.

It slayed him.

Because even as they collapsed onto the bed, Cain knew he couldn't have her. Not the way he wanted. Completely. Phoebe would want the same from him, and he could not give it.

Ever.

Sheltering the feelings in his heart was far better than seeing loathing in her eyes.

Cain stood at the foot of the bed, staring down at her as he buttoned his shirt. She'd slept all night without waking. Probably for the first time since Kreeg had ruined her life. While it pleased him, Cain knew they'd made a mistake.

He'd made the mistake.

He should have shown more willpower, he should have kept his distance. But with her, he had no will and he'd only himself to blame.

But Phoebe would be hurt. He hated himself for it already, yet she'd expect him to leave Nine Oaks and return to the life he had before Lily died.

He wouldn't. In that, nothing had changed.

His chest tightened, a knot locking around his heart. When she rolled to her side and smiled at him, Cain savored it for a moment, memorizing the look of pure contentment on her face.

"Good morning." She rose to her knees, naked and rosy and the temptation to have her again nearly stole his breath. He would never have enough of her and without asking, he knew she'd want more than he could give.

"You're dressed already?"

"I have work to do."

"Could I interest you in taking another day off?" On her knees, she reached, her fingertips dipping beneath his belt and tugging him closer.

"Phoebe, last night—"

"Was great."

"It was magnificent, however—"

Frowning, Phoebe let go and eased back, a horrible feeling skating over her spine. "However what?" She could feel the blow coming before it struck.

"I think this was a mistake."

Tension leaped into her and she snatched up the sheet, pulling it with her as she left the bed. "How can you say that?"

"Passion isn't everything."

"It's a damn good start and who says that's all there is? Don't you know how I feel about you?"

Please don't say more, he thought. *Please don't.*
"It wouldn't matter."

"Oh really? Why?"

"I won't leave Nine Oaks, Phoebe, and I know you're expecting me to now."

Angry heat flamed her face. "Don't tell me what I'm thinking or what I want, and yes, I do want you to leave here, but for your sake, not mine! Good God, you are so dense sometimes." She threw the sheet around her like a toga. "I want you to come back to the real world, Cain, for you. You're not happy and you won't be till you face what's out there." She gestured to the balcony. "And making love with you has nothing to do with it. You've hidden long enough. I know Lily did something to make you this way, and right now, I hate her for it."

Cain said nothing.

Phoebe felt it, that door slamming, the emotional shield closing him off from her.

And it hurt.

God, it hurt.

Her heart burned, her eyes seared and she blinked. "Damn you, Cain. It doesn't need to be like this."

Her tears destroyed him, each one cutting him to ribbons down to his soul. Cain wanted things to be different, wished to God that he'd followed his heart nine years ago and not his head. But right now, his head was clear. Staring into her teary eyes, he knew—his heart was breaking.

She moved toward the door.

"Phoebe."

"Go to hell, Cain." She stepped out the door and shut it behind herself.

I don't need to go to hell, Cain thought, staring at the empty room. *I'm in it.*

And he'd made it himself.

Phoebe hurried toward her rooms, covering her mouth, and wanting to scream *why!* Inside her room, she shut the door and fell back against it. The tears came, hard and mean, and she crumpled to the floor in a heap, and let them fall. She cried for the man Cain once was, for the one she'd glimpsed this week, and last night, for the passion they'd shared and never would share again.

He couldn't see a future, refused to see anything beyond the walls of Nine Oaks. Drawing him out had changed nothing and Phoebe told herself she had to face the fact that the past few days were merely a vacation from reality.

He's still in a damn cave, she thought.

Cain heard the chink of china and looked up as Benson deposited the tray on his desk with more force than necessary.

"Will there be anything else, sir?"

Cain frowned at his bitter tone. "No, Benson. Thank you." Yet Benson didn't move, staring down at him as if looking down his nose in disgust. "Have you something to say?" Cain asked.

"Yes, sir."

"And?"

"You're an ass, sir."

Cain's brows shot up.

"You have allowed that witch Lily to ruin your life yet again, and now you are also letting her ruin Miss Phoebe's."

"You've seen her?" Cain hadn't seen Phoebe in two days. They'd avoided each other when Cain wanted nothing more than to go to her. But he had nothing to say.

"Yes, I have. At present she is in the gym, sir, beating the stuffing out of a punching bag."

Cain scowled darkly. "Anything else, Benson, since you seem to be airing your feelings today?"

"Not anything I'd want repeated in civilized company, *sir.*" Benson spun around and left, shutting the door hard.

Cain threw down his pen and mashed a hand over his face. Great. He left his offices and headed to the gym where, as Benson said, she was going to town on a punching bag.

The instant he drew near, she stopped, met his gaze, then went back to pounding.

"Phoebe."

"I'd stand clear if I were you."

"I took advantage of you, and I'm sor—"

She stilled, glaring at him and cut him off with, "If you try to apologize for making love to me, I'm going to break something *very* expensive. And we took advantage of each other. And you know what?" She walked up to him breathing hard, sweating, and he wondered if he should duck. "I loved it. Every second of it. And I don't regret it."

"Neither do I!"

"Then why are you apologizing?" The pain and hurt in her eyes stung him again. He was right in doing this, he knew. She would not stay here, locked away, and he'd never expect her to. Cain could face Phoebe, but not the world beyond Nine Oaks. Not the crimes he'd committed.

"I've hurt you."

"You're hurting yourself and you're lying to yourself. Big, strong, rich and powerful Cain Blackmon, and you let some ghost haunt you?"

"And you're letting Kreeg haunt you," he threw back.

"Kreeg is not stopping me from enjoying life. He's stopping me from a good night's sleep." She lifted her gloved hand to her mouth and used her teeth to free the knots. Cain came to her, holding the glove and helping her.

"You're wasting your life."

"It's mine to waste."

She lifted her gaze to his. "And what about me, Cain? Do I mean nothing to you?"

His eyes flared. "You mean everything to me."

Somwhere in her heart, a spark lit. "Then tell me about Lily, about the rotting boat on the shore."

Cain went still as glass, his gaze riveted to her, but not seing her. "No."

"Why?"

"No!" He turned and left.

Phoebe sagged and threw the gloves across the room and snatched up a towel, wiping her face. She'd had free access to everything except the boats. Lily had died in a boating accident.

Refusing to let this go, she left the gym, listening for the sound of his voice, his footsteps. She found him on the back veranda, his hands on the stone rail, his shoulders stiff. His head was low, as if a great weight pushed it down.

"I understand your need to shut out the world, Cain. I did that. But now it's time to get back in and fight."

"Leave it alone, Phoebe. Please."

"Don't leave me, Cain," she said softly. He lifted

his gaze to hers. "You left me nine years ago. Don't do it again." Tears choked her throat, fracturing her voice.

She loved him. In that splintered moment, she knew it without a doubt.

"Phoebe, I can't. You don't know what I've done."

"Then tell me and let's work past it."

His ugly past pressured him to cut the ties and go back to the way things were before she entered his life again. He didn't want to. God, he wanted her to stay, to be a part of his life, just as she was a part of his heart.

She was the breath that moved each day along, he thought.

"Cain, talk to me."

"It's no use, Phoebe." She'd despise him and be gone anyway, he thought. "I can't give you what you want. I won't leave here and I won't ask you to stay.

"And if you did? What do you think I'd say?"

"It would be cruel to you, sweetheart." He passed a hand over her hair, cupped her jaw. "You're so vibrant and alive."

"And you were last night, too."

His lip twitched, and Cain gazed into her soulful eyes, and wanted to end his seclusion. "I will not leave here."

Her expression fell and she stepped back. "Then I will."

"What?"

"I'm leaving. In the morning."

"It's your choice." The heart-wrenching pain in his chest made his words soft, and as she turned away, Cain knew he was watching his one chance at something wonderful slip through his fingers.

She won't be here every day, a voice said. Cain wondered how he'd survive. How he'd breathe without her near.

Phoebe hung up the phone, old fear skating through her. She hugged herself, walking through the house without any direction. Beyond the walls a storm raged in tandem with her feelings.

"Who was on the phone?"

She stopped, refusing to look at Cain. "No one."

"Phoebe."

"Leave it alone. I don't need your help."

"I want to help." He reached for her, touching her shoulder and she flinched and whipped around to glare at him.

And Cain saw fear. He frowned. "Phoebe, tell me what's wrong? What's happened?"

"That was my lawyer. Or rather the one you hired. The trial starts tomorrow."

"That's good then. It will be over soon."

"He'll get off and it will never be over!"

She rushed away from him, leaving him standing in the foyer, watching her race up the stairs. Cain spun on his heels and went to his offices, dialing the lawyers. Phoebe refused to testify.

If she didn't, then Kreeg walked.

She'd spend her life looking over her shoulder in fear and want to hide from the world. *She'd become him.* He couldn't let that happen and he hurried to her suite, opening the doors without knocking.

"You have to testify."

"No, I don't."

"Phoebe, he committed a crime against you, you have to put him away."

"The evidence speaks for itself."

"But your testimony could clinch it."

"I can't," she cried.

Cain's heart softened, and he went to her, kneeling beside the chair, and forcing her to look at him.

"You're scared."

"I can't look at him, I can't. He hurt me, he touched me. And I know he'll have the best lawyers and money, and get off. I'm nobody."

"No, you're not. You can do this."

She shook her head, and Cain saw her recovery in the last weeks crumbling. "You can't hide from it. You'll never be safe if you don't put him away." He swallowed hard. "And then you'll turn into me."

She met his gaze. "That's not so bad."

"Yes, it is." His expression darkened. "And I won't allow it."

"And just how will you do that?"

"I'll go with you."

Her eyes flared wide. "What?"

Cain took a deep breath before he said, "I'll escort you to the trial and stay right beside you."

She was silent for a moment as his words hit her. He'd leave Nine Oaks? He'd break a five-year seclusion for her? "Do you realize what your appearance in public will do? It will cause more stir than the trial."

"Then attention will be on me and not you, right?"

"Why? Why would you do this?"

"I want you to feel safe again, Phoebe, and if you don't go and tell the jury what he did to you, then he could walk away and do the same thing to another woman." Or to her again, he thought, but knew he'd never let that happen.

"Cain." Tears slid down her cheek.

"I'll be with you, baby. I swear, I'll protect you."

She fell into his arms, clinging tightly, touched beyond thought, beyond breathing. Over her shoulder Cain squeezed his eyes shut, realizing he wanted Phoebe's happiness more than he did his own.

Ten

When Cain Blackmon stepped back into the real world, he did it with style, Phoebe thought. A chopper had landed on the Nine Oaks front lawn, and flew them to the airport where they boarded a Gulfstream jet and headed toward California for the trial.

"You're gawking," he said with a gentle smile.

She kept looking around the lush cabin. "You've never used this, have you?"

"Suzannah does, and my other employees. But no, I haven't."

But he was using it for her.

The impact of what he was doing hit her all over

again. He left five years of seclusion behind to be with her now. To shield her. And if she loved him before, she loved him more today. He met her gaze, a tiny frown knitting his brow and she wondered if he knew she'd fallen in love with him.

"I hate flying by the way."

"You've done admirably well considering we're landing."

The instant they were out of the jet, they were besieged.

"Word's out you're here," she said and he simply smiled tenderly down at her and guided her to the limousine. She saw another side of him, a man who commanded the world around him, and expected to be obeyed. Cameras flashed, people shouted, and yet she felt safe and guarded in a mad crowd of onlookers. Cain said nothing, refusing to respond to a single question even when they were offensive and cruel. His arm around her was a comforting shelter as he escorted her into the courthouse and to her lawyers.

She stilled when she saw Kreeg enter, and that smug smile of his fell when his gaze landed on Cain. He went pale and turned to his attorneys, whispering furiously.

Phoebe looked up at Cain. His expression was murderous as he stared at Kreeg. She nudged him and when he met her gaze, the look evaporated, replaced by a smile.

Bending to kiss her cheek, he whispered, "Be brave. I'm right here. He can't touch you anymore."

The trial proceeded, evidence produced and debated. The lawyers Cain hired were magnificent, and the private detective shed light on Kreeg's past. This wasn't the first time he'd tormented a woman, and a parade of victims on the stand confirmed it. Phoebe's stomach clenched when she had to take the stand, yet she kept her gaze on Cain. He was her anchor, and she gathered strength from him, his encouraging smile, and when Kreeg's lawyers tried to destroy her, they failed.

Then the jury was sequestered. Cain had taken a suite in a nearby hotel and posted guards around the clock to keep the press and the curious away. Watching him take control of the situation, Phoebe didn't say much. She was grateful for his strength.

"Phoebe, you should rest."

She looked up from her perch on the sofa. "I want it to be over."

"It will be." He looked at his watch.

"What's taking so long? It's been a while," she said.

"No, it hasn't. They are deciding a man's future. I'm just wondering where dinner is."

That made her smile, and the corners of his mouth lifted in tandem. He came to sit down beside her.

"Thank you," she said.

"You're welcome."

"It wasn't so hard, was it?"

He thought for a second. "I didn't seclude myself because of the press and nosy people, Phoebe. I secluded myself because I didn't want to be near anyone and inflict my moods on them."

"Well, I've seen some of those moods. They aren't so bad."

He eyed her, knowing the truth.

"Well, you've been wonderful to me," she said.

He smirked to himself. "Yes well, you're hard to resist and difficult to keep away."

"Are you saying I'm pushy?"

"Oh hell, yes."

She laughed and Cain grinned. "Admit it, you've had fun," she said.

"Nah, you'll get an ego."

She gave him a playful shove and unwound her body from the tight curl in the corner of the sofa. "You know the ugly parts of my life, Cain. When will you tell me yours?"

Cain leaned forward and clasped his hands, staring at them. "Phoebe, please understand." Cain could feel the battle boiling inside him, sudden and harsh at the first thought of his crime. The power of guilt was an ugly creature and it had badgered him for years.

"Cain, please."

He didn't answer, and Phoebe could see the emotion simmering under his expression.

"I can't understand any of it, if I don't know the truth."

He rounded on her, his expression contorted in guilt. "You want the truth? Are you sure?"

"Yes, I do."

"I killed my wife, Phoebe. Is that truth enough?"

She reared back. "What? No, that can't be true."

"I let her go out on a boat when I knew she wasn't skilled enough to sail!" He started to stand.

Phoebe pushed him back down. "Whoa, wait a second." She touched his face, making him look at her and his dark, tortured stare broke her heart. "Take a breath."

He did, pushing his fingers through his hair and knowing it was now or never. Cain realized he was simply postponing the inevitable, but he didn't want to lose her now.

"I told you I married her because she carried my child. I didn't love her and I never claimed to love her. She was a weekend in my life that ruined both our lives."

"But she loved you, didn't she?"

"Yes. God, it killed me to see it in her eyes all the time. When she lost the child, I tried to make it work.

But we were strangers in the same house. She wanted me to love her and I couldn't." He looked at Phoebe. "I tried, but it wasn't there." Not like it is for you, he thought, and looked away. "And after a couple of months, she knew it never would be. Her feelings turned to hate and anger, and we fought over everything. I talked to my lawyer about filing for divorce. I meant to tell her that night, but she learned it by eavesdropping. We had a terrible fight, said things to each other that were cruel."

"How did she die on the boat?"

"After the fight, she went outside. I knew she was on the property from the cameras and staff. I thought she'd cool off and we could at least part like adults, be civil. She went off like that a lot when we'd argue, but she was gone a long time. So I went to look for her. She was in the boat, just sitting in it. It was tied to the dock and she shouted at me to leave her alone."

Cain rubbed his mouth, then clasped his hands again. He'd never let himself think of that night for long, but now it unfolded in his mind.

"I didn't think she'd take the boat out. She wasn't a skilled sailor, and she knew it!"

"Was there a storm or something? The river is wide, but it's pretty calm."

"No, not at first. The sun was setting and it started to rain, but nothing bad. When she didn't come back near sundown, I went looking again. That's when I realized she'd taken the boat out." He glanced at her. "It wasn't the first time she did something like that to get my attention. So I called the sea rescue, and went looking for her in the speedboat. But even the sea rescue couldn't spot the boat with floodlights. She just vanished." He flopped back into the cushions. "I'd hoped she drew in downriver somewhere south."

"She didn't."

He shook his head. "The rain worsened. I didn't come in, just drifted up and down the shore. I stayed out there all night and in the morning, I found the boat. Then her."

Phoebe could only imagine what he'd felt at that moment, and knew without asking he'd carried that tortured reminder with him ever since.

"Cain, she was skilled enough to bring it in, wasn't she?"

"I don't know." He pushed off the sofa and paced. "No, I know she wasn't. I let her go out on that boat and she died."

"Oh my God. You blame yourself for her death?"

His gaze slammed into hers. "I killed her! I could have stopped her, carried her back into the house, anything to keep her from sailing. I destroyed her, Phoebe. I couldn't love her and it destroyed her."

"Wait a minute, Lily was a grown woman, and she knew her skill level." She stood before him, gripping his arms, wanting him to hear her so badly. "*She* knew she couldn't sail and yet she did. In a storm. It was all intentional. She took that boat out to kill herself!"

Cain shook his head. "Don't you think I want to believe that? She said, 'I'll see you later, I'll come in a minute.' She didn't mean to…"

"Die?"

"Yes. What did the coroner say?"

"No injuries, a drowning."

"She could swim?"

"Yes."

"Then she didn't want to."

"I should have forced her inside. I should have made her come back."

"You should have loved her, isn't that what you're saying?"

He crumpled before her eyes, his shoulders drooping, his head bowing.

"Oh, Cain." She brushed her mouth over his, her throat going tight. "Oh honey, you can't force love when it's not there."

He lifted his gaze to her.

"There's no crime in not loving her. There is when you let it keep *you* from loving."

His features tightened, and he bent, calling her name. Before their lips touched, the phone rang.

Cain straightened, and went to answer it.

Phoebe hugged herself, watching his expression. He gave nothing away as he hung up. "The jury is in," he said. "Let's go." .

Cain whisked her away from the courthouse so fast she didn't have time to think about anything but that she was free, and Kreeg was behind bars for a very long time.

On the plane Cain didn't talk, and barely looked at her. It hurt that he wouldn't look at her, yet Phoebe left him to his thoughts. She could see his torment, as if he was reliving his wife's death. When the plane touched down, he looked up as if just realizing he'd been silent for so long. He apologized and within an hour, she was walking back into Nine Oaks.

On the stairs, she looked down at him. "Cain."

"I'll see you in the morning."

Phoebe's heart broke. He didn't have to say it. He was closing himself off. Nothing she'd said had made a difference, and he wasn't letting her share his burden. Now he was letting her go.

"I can't stay here anymore."

He jerked a look up at her. "Yes, you can go home now. You're safe."

"Oh Cain. This is my home." His features went taut. "Don't you know? You have my heart." Her voice broke. "My very soul. And that will never change, but I can't stay with a man who is too trapped in useless guilt to see a future."

His features tightened. "Phoebe, please."

"No, Cain, it doesn't have to be this way. Open your eyes! You didn't do anything wrong! Except give a ghost power over you."

His eyes narrowed, and yet Phoebe simply sighed and turned away. She loved him. She'd always loved him, she realized. And now, she would lose him to a woman who'd been dead for five years.

She came to him like soft fragrance on the breeze, stirring his senses, shifting the air surrounding him.

Cain felt her touch before he heard her whisper his name. He shifted on the bed and saw an image that would stay with him for a lifetime—Phoebe, naked and ethereal, sliding onto his bed and into his arms.

Cain didn't think, didn't question, and when she tipped her head back, meeting his gaze, touching his face, she gave no answers. Then he kissed her, a deep slow kiss of love and passion. The fast heat and demand they'd felt before was tamed. Now the need to show and revere overtook him. In the back of his mind, Cain knew this would be the last time he touched Phoebe.

His patience showed in his touch, in the way he stirred her body. Phoebe took what she wanted for herself, sliding down his body to pleasure him like no other. Cain groaned and yanked her up to him, a look full of sensual promise lighting her heart. He tasted her body, claimed it as he had never done before, with complete possession, taking part of her soul with every kiss.

His hands played over her skin, memorizing her shape, his mouth drawing on her nipples, teeth scraping erotically over the swells of her breasts and lower. Then he spread her wide, and gripped her hips, lifting her to his mouth.

He laved at her center, making her cry out softly, making her squirm for more. Her beauty enthralled him, burned into his mind and still, he tasted her, toyed with her pleasure. It was his, he owned it, he wanted no man to do this to her. Ever. She was his, he thought. No matter what he felt or said, Phoebe was his.

And he showed her, bringing her to peak after peak, skillfully letting her dangle on the edge, then releasing her and covering her body with his.

She spread herself for him and Cain slid smoothly inside her warm wet center. The heat of her nearly undid him and he moved slowly, his tempo measured, her desire blossoming. He wanted to savor each sensation, the womanly muscles gripping and flexing on him, the short gasps tumbling from her lips. He pushed and withdrew, watching her eyes flare, her heart in her beautiful face.

Cain's throat locked and he could barely breathe, knowing this was the last time, and knowing he would die without her in his life.

He groaned her name as he kissed her, quickening, and she clung to him, her limbs wrapped tightly. The spiral of heat climbed as their bodies took control in a powerful rush to find the summit together.

Then it came, a swell of throbbing skin and heated kisses. His tongue plunged into her mouth as his body thrust hard into her. She whispered his name, he called hers and threw his head back as the tight pulse of their climax exploded and fused between them.

The moment suspended, heartbeats matched, passion spreading out like ribbons to tie them together. Cain felt everything with an odd clarity and when he looked down at her, she was smiling, her teary eyes so somber and heartbreaking. Cain felt his heart shatter.

"Don't leave," he said, dragging her to his side. "Don't."

She said nothing, stroking his face, his hair, and then cradling him to her breast.

Cain felt emotion grab him, its powerful surge pulling him in, and he wanted it, desperate to latch on tight. But something else tugged at him, the old feelings, old pain, and it wasn't till he was drifting off to sleep that he realized the chance of his life beckoned, and his ties to his past were only tattered fringes in his mind.

Cain stood several yards from the shore and tossed a match on the ruined sailboat. The dry, old wood flamed quickly and he sat on the ground, watching it burn to ashes.

He let himself be burdened by guilt. When he woke alone this morning, the scent of Phoebe lingered, reminding him what he was losing for the sake of a ghost.

It wasn't so much her words that changed him, it was realizing he hadn't thought of Lily in weeks, not in the way he had in the past. Now she was an old memory he tried to keep alive for all the wrong reasons.

He'd made a mistake by trying to love someone he couldn't. He bore the burden of giving Lily hope when he should have ended their relationship quickly. He would not shoulder the blame any longer.

Not at the cost of his love for Phoebe.

I'm done here, he thought.

Free. Down to his soul.

The wood popped and hissed as Cain let out a deep breath. He'd known he would come to this place, this moment, someday, but it took Phoebe's resilience to make him step this close to his past. She gave him the strength, his love for her overshadowing Lily.

Ashes spiraled toward the sky and he smiled. With it, went his past. His guilt.

Then he heard the sound of an engine and twisted to look toward the house. In the distance, he could see figures near the garages—Benson, Willis, Mr. Dobbs.

And Phoebe.

Cain jumped to his feet, glanced at the dying embers, then ran toward the house.

She was leaving.

Phoebe hugged Benson and tried to hide her tears as she walked to her Jeep. The others departed quickly, and she was opening the door when she heard her name and turned. First she saw the trail of smoke spiraling toward the sky, then Cain walking briskly toward her.

Instantly she noticed something different about him.

"I've never seen you dress like that." His worn jeans molded his body, the T-shirt snug over his wide chest, but it was the ease of his stride, the softness in his moves that caught her in the chest.

"I thought it was time I left some things behind, and buried them forever."

Phoebe's heartbeat skipped and stuttered. "What things?"

He advanced, his steps determined. "The ogre, the guilt. I needed room for other feelings."

"Oh, really?"

He grinned. "God, I love it when you get that sass in your look."

Phoebe's breath caught as he walked right up to her and cradled her face in his cool hands.

"Don't leave me."

Tears blurred his image. "I can't stay here locked away with you."

"Then don't. Open more doors with me." She started to speak, but he kept talking. "Shh, listen to me. I've been an idiot." Her lips quivered at that. "I let myself be trapped, I made my own life more miserable, and yet, you stuck around, you dragged me out of that dark place. Don't give up on us now. After all we've been through, please don't."

She covered his hands. "Oh, Cain."

He swallowed, gazing deeply into her green eyes. "I need you so much I can't breathe without you. You're my life. I love you, Phoebe DeLongpree, *I love you.*"

"Cain." Her breath caught and a tear fell. "I love you, too. I think I have for years."

He smiled, his own eyes burning as he thanked God for her. The other half of his soul. "Stay with me. Make a life with me. Have babies with me." He brushed his mouth to hers. "Marry me, Phoebe. Marry me, please."

She didn't hesitate. "Yes, yes."

"Ahh," he said. "Thank God." He captured her mouth, lifting her off her feet and crushing her in his arms. He peppered her face in kisses and she begged for more, laughing. They tumbled to the grass, the dogs rushing to leap and bound over them and Cain flopped to his back, Phoebe in his arms. She stared down at him, her fingers trailing lightly across his brow.

"I love you," he said, his gaze sketching her face, the sunlight glittering in her hair.

A happy tear trickled down her cheek. "Took you long enough."

He laughed and squeezed her and smiled, and with her nestled at his side on the sun-kissed grass, peace settled over them, wrapping them in a bright future.

Cain kissed the top of her head, and could almost feel his ancestors staring down at them, pleased that Nine Oaks was alive with hope again, that laughter would fill its rooms and shower endless Southern nights with a love that would span centuries.

* * * * *

If you enjoyed what you just read,
then we've got an offer you can't resist!

Take 2 bestselling
love stories FREE!

Plus get a FREE surprise gift!

Clip this page and mail it to Silhouette Reader Service™

IN U.S.A.	**IN CANADA**
3010 Walden Ave.	P.O. Box 609
P.O. Box 1867	Fort Erie, Ontario
Buffalo, N.Y. 14240-1867	L2A 5X3

YES! Please send me 2 free Silhouette Desire® novels and my free surprise gift. After receiving them, if I don't wish to receive anymore, I can return the shipping statement marked cancel. If I don't cancel, I will receive 6 brand-new novels every month, before they're available in stores! In the U.S.A., bill me at the bargain price of $3.80 plus 25¢ shipping and handling per book and applicable sales tax, if any*. In Canada, bill me at the bargain price of $4.47 plus 25¢ shipping and handling per book and applicable taxes**. That's the complete price and a savings of at least 10% off the cover prices—what a great deal! I understand that accepting the 2 free books and gift places me under no obligation ever to buy any books. I can always return a shipment and cancel at any time. Even if I never buy another book from Silhouette, the 2 free books and gift are mine to keep forever.

225 SDN DZ9F
326 SDN DZ9G

Name	(PLEASE PRINT)	
Address	Apt.#	
City	State/Prov.	Zip/Postal Code

Not valid to current Silhouette Desire® subscribers.

Want to try two free books from another series?
Call 1-800-873-8635 or visit www.morefreebooks.com.

* Terms and prices subject to change without notice. Sales tax applicable in N.Y.
** Canadian residents will be charged applicable provincial taxes and GST.
  All orders subject to approval. Offer limited to one per household.
  ® are registered trademarks owned and used by the trademark owner and or its licensee.

DES04R   ©2004 Harlequin Enterprises Limited

Coming in November
from Silhouette Desire

DYNASTIES : THE ASHTONS

*A family built on lies…brought together
by dark, passionate secrets*

continues with

SAVOR THE SEDUCTION

by Laura Wright

Grant Ashton came
to Napa Valley to discover the truth
about his family…but found so much
more. Was Anna Sheridan, a woman
battling her own demons, the answer
to all Grant's desires?

*Available this November wherever
Silhouette books are sold.*

Silhouette® Desire®

A violent storm.

A warm cabin.

One bed…for two strangers
stranded overnight.

Author

Bronwyn Jameson's

latest PRINCES OF THE OUTBACK novel
will sweep you off your feet and into
a world of privilege and passion!

Don't miss

The Ruthless Groom

Silhouette Desire #1691
Available November 2005

Only from Silhouette Books!

COMING NEXT MONTH

#1687 SAVOR THE SEDUCTION—Laura Wright
Dynasties: The Ashtons
Scandals had rocked his family but only one woman was able to shake him to the core.

#1688 BOSS MAN—Diana Palmer
Long, Tall Texans
This tough-as-leather attorney never looked twice at his dedicated assistant…until now!

#1689 HIGHLY COMPROMISED POSITION—Sara Orwig
Texas Cattleman's Club: The Secret Diary
How could she have known the sexy stranger who fathered her child was her family's sworn enemy?

#1690 THE CHASE IS ON—Brenda Jackson
The Westmorelands
His lovely new neighbor was a sweet temptation this confirmed bachelor couldn't resist.

#1691 THE RUTHLESS GROOM—Bronwyn Jameson
Princes of the Outback
She delivered the news that his bride-to-be had run away…never expecting to be next on his "to wed" list.

#1692 MISTLETOE MANEUVERS—Margaret Alison
Mixing business with pleasure could only lead to a hostile takeover…and a whole lot of passion.

SDCNM1005